I0630901

Love Me Wild

A Warriors of Maida Novella

Renee Field

Published by Renee Field, 2018.

LOVE ME WILD

First edition. February 4, 2018.

ISBN: 978-1393814559

Written by Renee Field.

Chapter One

Rowena shivered as she placed the test tube into the cycle-tron, hoping the results would be wrong. Deep down, she knew they wouldn't be. Ten minutes later, the cycle was complete. The tube was bright blue. The results were positive, she had the Maida curse—she was fertile. Rowena cringed, knowing what was to come.

Even though she was Maida's top biologist, she couldn't halt years of evolution. For the first time in her life, she wished to be like her sister, Tyrana—sterile. *Then my life would be my own.* How she envied her sister's freedom of choice.

A century ago, after the religious wars ceased, it was too late for the Maida people. While radioactive weapons had destroyed only a small number of islands, the effect was all-encompassing. The ions from those weapons had sealed themselves deep within the genetic sequence of their race.

When it became apparent only a handful of women and men were fertile, keeping their race alive became paramount. Maida women able to conceive became cherished. After the last Great War, thirteen fertile women formed the Supreme High Fertility Council—to ensure the continuation of their species.

The Maida curse, as it became known by fertile women, was a double-edged sword. Once a woman was able to conceive, her body and mind didn't matter—all she craved was sex. If she didn't have sex with a fertile man, she went insane within days.

Talk about harsh reality, thought Rowena. Worse was the keen knowledge that once she had sex, the disease that had been eating away at her brain cells at the molecular level would be passed to the man.

In a fit of rage, Rowena threw the tube across the room. She watched with smug satisfaction as it smashed into a thousand pieces, the blue liquid staining the white marble floor. She was not going to wipe it up. Let it stain. She felt like a chain had been placed around her neck.

"What was that noise?" yelled her mother, rushing into the room with two guards in tow.

Realizing the stupidity of her actions, she fought the urge to yell at her mother—Faydon, Her Majesty, Ruler of the Supreme High Fertility Council. Her mother, like her aunts who sat on the Council, viewed their job as paramount. Rowena thought of them as a nuisance. Now however, she was in for it.

"What were you doing, Rowena?"

Her mother's eyes took in the smashed test tube and blue liquid with a quick calculated glance. Rowena watched as the liquid tried its best to seep under a storage cabinet. *That's exactly what I'd like to do. Hide. Become invisible. Instead, I'm left to confront the last person I want to be near.*

Sighing, she plunked herself down on one of the tall, uncomfortable steel lab stools and replied, "Nothing."

"Your Majesty," said Thelma.

Traitor. She watched through narrowed lids as her mother's most trusted friend and advisor ushered her mother over to examine the floor.

"Is it true, Rowena?"

Hope highlighted her mother's pale features. Rowena nodded in exasperation. She was too exhausted to formulate a lie or a plan to get her out of the mess she knew she was in.

"Quick, we must call the Council. Oh Rowena, this is too good. Your time has come. We had thought..."

Rowena watched as her mother struggled for the proper words. Not that she had to. She knew what her mother was going to say. She had thought Rowena, at the age of twenty-three Maida cycles, was sterile like her other daughter.

All my prayers to the Mother Saint have been for naught. She didn't listen to one word I said. I don't want to be fertile. This is an interruption in my life I most certainly do not need.

Rowena tried hard to compose herself as her mother ushered the guards out of the room to do her bidding. Her nerves were frayed and her emotions were running high. *The joys of what elevated hormones will do to you. Too bad they hadn't come up with a pill to cure that.*

"Your aunts will be very excited," her mother said, moving closer to give her an embrace.

It was an awkward moment for both mother and daughter who were not used to public, or private, displays of affection. Still though, Rowena acknowledged a small part of her was pleased that her mother seemed happy. *Just how long will this last?*

"How many days?" asked Thelma, flanking her other side.

Rowena's eyes narrowed, knowing that the happy moment with her mother was about to expire. "Two."

"What!"

The screech that went through the lab vibrated the crystal beakers. *Here it comes.* She gripped the steel edges of the stool tighter. Preparing herself for the worst, she was surprised to hear her mother take a long breath in to compose herself. *Maybe she'll ignore this.*

"You will make your choice tonight," demanded her mother, in the no-nonsense tone of voice Rowena knew from experience couldn't be deterred.

Rowena watched as her mother huffed, picked up her bright purple robes and marched out of the lab. Then, and only then, did Thelma place a soothing hand on her shoulder.

"Why must you do everything the hard way?"

It wasn't a question her mother's advisor expected an answer to. Rowena bowed her head in despair, as Thelma strode after her mother. *This is stupid. I will not choose. I will not. She can't make me...can she?*

3

Rowena knew the answer already. She had no choice. Her mother would make her choose, because if she didn't Rowena would go insane within days. The desire, passion, ache...*whatever* the Supreme High Fertility Council called it, would systematically eat away her mental balance. Why women viewed fertility as a blessing she couldn't fathom.

That was why she had tried desperately to ignore what was happening to her body. Part of the other reason was work, but that was an excuse. She had sensed the changes taking place, as much as she tried to ignore them.

After all, no woman growing up on the continent called Maida was innocent to their body's biology. At first though, she had naïvely thought she might be coming down with a bout of the Castima flu, but three days later her symptoms became more acute. First came the cramps in her side, followed by tender breasts. Today her nipples were so sensitive that even wearing the light fire-resistant lab coat caused them to ache with a need that was indescribable.

A slow pulsing throb between her legs made her constantly squirm on the lab stool. She had an overwhelming urge to shamelessly rub her body up and down a hard column to appease the unknown itch burning under her skin.

She was moody and weepy, two emotions she had never experienced before. Even at a young age, she took pride in her calm, rational outlook, often chiding her older sister for her childish and irresponsible behavior. Now these strange emotions left her feeling vulnerable.

If her calculations were correct, she had two days before the disease that was triggered when her body became fertile caused her brain cells to decay. It was a small window of time to adjust to the idea she would be forced to give up her high-profile job and rut with a man she would claim solely for his fertile seed.

It was a cruel twist to the curse that it was a man's fertile seed that would trigger the chemical response in her body, systematically killing the disease. By rutting with a so-called lucky man, who had the privilege of being selected by her during the Pleasure Seeking selection, the disease was passed to him. Unfortunately for the man, there was no cure and they usually went quickly insane.

Knowing what was to come repulsed her. The entire concept was disgusting. She couldn't believe her luck.

Tonight her mother would make her choose a bed partner. Of that she was certain. After all, with two daughters, one of whom was sterile, she, Rowena, was the only female to keep their lineage alive. She almost choked on that thought.

Like the other handful of fertile women, she would be paraded through the Council—given a joyous "coming out" ceremony. Later today, she would undergo the dreaded inspection. Nothing would be left untouched.

Her body—a vessel to carry forth the next Maida generation—would no longer be her own. The final coup de grace was the injection. The pheromones would stream into her blood, heightening her already feverishly high levels of estrogen, forcing her to choose a mate. Her scientific mind would no longer function. She would be a slave to lust and the need to mate.

The knowledge she'd have to choose a mate and be forced to rut the whole blasted night away caused her to cringe. She had stupidly assumed she was too old—that had been a kernel of hope. Fertility often came late to Maida women. The only reason she knew her sister, Tyrana, was sterile was because at twenty-eight cycles she had demanded the sterility test so she could have fun with her life.

Something she liked to point out to Rowena countless times in any given day as she tried to get her to join in one of her famously explicit sexual romps. However, until either the curse hit her or she, too, took the sterility test, she had to remain a virgin. It was a hard-and-fast rule the Supreme High Fertility Council imposed on its female protectorates.

Why Tyrana and not me? Rowena fervently wished she could exchange her body with her sister's.

She groaned loudly, hating that her fertility cycle had caught up with her. After being on her feet for the past twelve hours trying to figure out the latest batch of blood work that had been sent to her from the Fourth Colony, the last thing she wanted was this.

She was at least thankful the blood had been sent to her. The challenge of figuring out why more men from the Fourth Colony were becoming sterile appealed to her. The colony was located at the furthest perimeter of Maida territory bordering the All Saints Lakes. The males there, like Maida men everywhere, either worked in the small specialized labor camps or as domestics inside the business centers operated by women.

Rowena shivered as a new realization hit her. Becoming fertile meant her mother would groom her to take over her seat on the Supreme High Fertility Council which meant living her life as a "proper" Maida mother. Sex for pleasure would be out of the question. Sex for procreation was the cardinal rule once she joined the Council. Each time the Maida curse came upon her, she would be forced to choose a fertile male to ensure future Maida children on the planet Alvaron.

It was at times like this that she hated her male ancestors for what they did to the planet. Legend went that at the end of the last religious war, Maida men were stripped of all their weapons and toys. Defeated in body, spirit and soul, it was the women who stepped forward to ensure the future of their race. Without their courage, Maida civilization would have fallen to either the wilds of the dark woods or the waters that were slowly rising on Alvaron.

Giving up is what cowards do. Rowena came from a long line of courageous women and she would not give up. For the past five years, she had worked day and night in an attempt to find a cure for the dreaded Maida curse.

She grimaced while struggling to ignore the steady pulse that rippled through her core. Her panties felt wet with desire and her nipples had pebbled simply from the feel of her lab coat. She fought to assert calm over her body's biological demands.

"Rowena, you must come with us," commanded Thelma, stepping back inside the lab.

She scowled. The lab had always been her sanctuary. Now, however, the blue liquid pooling next to the storage cabinet was a stark reminder, almost a slap in the face, that scientific reasoning had nothing over biology any day.

Plus she was hungry. Her body lately had taken on strange cravings. *To think I'm not even pregnant yet and I'm craving food.* Thinking of food caused her mouth to salivate as she envisioned eating a noonday feast of salted teasers, the fish harvested in the aquamarine park, and pickled fester fruit which had come into season in the orchard greenhouse. A large rumble by her stomach told her she was famished.

"A meal awaits you, Rowena," said Thelma, giving her a slight smile. "And after you've had your fill, we will begin the preparations for the Pleasure Seeking selection."

Being reminded of that immediately caused her to lose her appetite. After her noonday feast, Rowena knew her life would never be the same again. She longed to stay within the safe confines of her lab, but that would be impossible.

To further the Maida race, she would be forced by the Council to undergo the Pleasure Seeking selection. Tonight she'd spread her legs so the man she chose could plunge his cock straight into her already wet pussy, all so she could live and conceive a child. That thought brought uncharacteristic tears to fill her eyes. She fought hard to keep them from brimming over.

Work is what I understand and can get my head around. If my sister were here, she'd say that head was something I most certainly am going to give tonight. She cringed, hating the erotic thought that popped into her mind.

Chapter Two

Tulon scowled as another bowl of pickled fester fruit passed his way. He forced the bitter round fruit into his body, already hating that it had come into season. *What I wouldn't give for fresh greens.*

"What some more, boy?" the female guard asked as she eyed him up and down like he was dessert.

He said nothing. He knew from past experience that it was better for him when he didn't speak. His voice aggravated the guards. After two years in the forced labor camp, Tulon had learned his lesson, somewhat. Privately he thought, *Bitch!*

Women disgusted him. Well, that wasn't entirely true. Mostly it was these women, the ugly she-men who had captured him, who made him want to puke. His mother, sister and clan women he understood. These ones, well, for the past twenty-four months he had thought of them as something else. They certainly looked alien to him and they were more brutish than he could ever have imagined a female capable of being.

Inwardly, he cursed at himself. *Stupid! I should have known better.* He never should have left the safety of the Dark Forest. Not that he had any choice in the matter. It was either expulsion or death. He had chosen the former. Now he was second-guessing his choice.

It wasn't as if the hard labor was all that difficult or physically draining to him. It was the nights. He was sick and tired of having to rut with the guards, acting all the while like he was enjoying it. He didn't. These women were nothing like the gentle, fun-loving creatures of his kind. They were large, dirt-ugly and stank.

"Are you going to eat that, 7653?" asked the man sitting next to him on the soft, plush cushions.

Having no name rankled Tulon the most. Without it he felt lost, alienated, as if he didn't matter. *Maybe I don't.*

He recalled vividly how the *thrush*—the transformation into a mature Centaur—had changed him for life. It hadn't been welcomed by his clan. Hence the banishment. Hence his imprisonment. Well, truthfully, that had been his own stupidity.

He had traveled almost half a moon through the Dark Forest, farther than any of his kind had dared to venture before. Food had grown scarcer with each passing day, but Tulon couldn't turn back. He didn't dare. If he did, his younger brother would also be forced from the herd. Tulon knew that meant certain death for his sibling, so under the watchful eye of his mother, he had trotted away.

No, his mother's mate, Rython, would have enjoyed that too much. His mother, Shylah, had taken Rython as her mate only after Tulon's father had died. At that time, she had already been expecting, so Rython hadn't been able to mate with his mother. After the birth of the twins, since all females nurse their young for up to six years, Rython had only grown more cantankerous because his mother hadn't come into heat or wanted to rut.

At first, Tulon had sympathized with him. However, he came to realize Rython could be cruel as well as vindictive. Rython hated him. The reason was simple.

He, Tulon, looked too much like his mother's previous mate. He bore the same dark markings, long black mane and coat and he was quick on his feet. So when the *thrush* had finally come to him and the change had happened, it had been the perfect excuse for Rython to expel him. Change was not something any of his kind liked.

The fair-haired man coughed, bringing Tulon back to the present.

"It's yours." He handed the pickled fester fruit to the man. He tried to recall the man's identification number, but it was no use. All the men looked the same to him. They were short, fair-haired, blue-eyed and talked way too much for his liking.

Countless nights, after being forced to fuck sometimes up to four female guards, he had come back to his rest cushions, only to toss and turn as he tried to drown out the sounds of the men pleasing each other.

Until his capture two years ago, he hadn't known that type of pleasure existed. Enlightened as he tried to be, it wasn't something for him. That he'd made perfectly clear to the first male who had attempted to befriend him. As bad as the female guards were, they would have to do for now.

A second platter of pickled fruit was passed his way by another fair-haired man. Tulon's mouth puckered. He didn't think he could stomach another pickled anything today. *By the Saints, why must they pickle their fruit and vegetables?* The idea was abhorrent to him. The gifts from the blessed Saints should be eaten as they were.

A loud clang of the door told him the guards were back. He forced a fake smile as two of the fattest guards waddled in.

"Take him, and him, and him," said the shorter of the two fat guards, as she pointed at three fair-haired men, who were now smiling from ear to ear.

"What about him?" asked the second guard.

Tulon didn't even bother to look up. He knew they were pointing at him. After a brief but heated discussion he too was ushered into the lineup.

So much for sleep tonight. He forced his muscles to relax and accept the metal collar around his neck. The collar was a control mechanism and every cell within his being rebelled at it. It was a test of his worth he could force himself to obey.

"You're sure Her Majesty won't mind?" asked the guard, poking him in the back, forcing him to move forward.

"She said to bring all the fertile men...and every test we've done on him has come back positive, so I don't think we're doing anything wrong," admonished the other guard.

"Yeah, but he's, well...he's different."

"Oh, you mean *that* different." The guard cackled loudly.

Tulon cringed, wanting to hit both women. That, too, was a new notion for him—wanting to physically hurt a woman. Women were to be cherished, loved and pleasured. The idea of doing anything less than to please a woman was viewed as a weakness in a Centaur.

Then again, maybe I'm no longer a Centaur after all. Before the *thrush*, he would have claimed being Centaur with pride. After the *thrush*, when all his powers came to the forefront, he wasn't so sure. All he knew for certain was, after that night when pain had sliced into his body and mind, passing him the knowledge of his kind, something had gone horribly wrong.

When he awoke, the intense knowledge of the magic had briefly flashed inside his being, but parts of it had remained hidden. He no longer knew what he was. He most certainly didn't like what he had become—either man or stallion, but never Centaur...never both, again.

The guards' laughter grated his sensitive hearing. He knew full well what they were chuckling about. His blasted cock. Even limp, which thankfully it was now, it was thick and long, much longer than the puny things stuck between the legs of the fair-haired ones. When desire swamped his senses, it tripled in thickness and length, hence his notoriety among the female guards.

"Want to go one more round before you leave us, Mighty Man?" challenged a guard, her putrid breath causing him to almost gag.

Mighty Man was their nickname for his shaft. Why they would give it a nickname mystified him.

"He can't...we don't have much time. He's got to be purified by tonight," answered the guard at the front, eyeing him lewdly in a sinful attempt to whet his appetite.

Tulon kept his head down, wondering what he was in for now.

Chapter Three

Inwardly, Rowena fumed. The inspection had been worse than she had ever imagined. *Why don't women talk about it? Are they, like me, too mortified to recall in graphic detail what had been done to their body—all in the name of fertility?*

First she had to enter the side Council chamber naked. Not a stitch of clothing. *Nothing.* Then she had been strapped to an examination table. Her ankles had been locked in place and her legs had been forced open. Her arms had been tied high above her head. Two of her aunts had come in, which had been mortifying. She was at least thankful her mother had chosen not to attend.

She shivered, recalling the highly barbaric ritual she had been put through. She tried finding one redeeming quality about the entire bizarre thing. When nothing popped to mind, she tried to stop the images of what had happened next.

One aunt had pinched both of her nipples so hard she had yelled out in pain, while another had wedged a large rubbery thing straight into her pussy. Rowena wasn't sure what had hurt more. Her highly sensitive nipples or the rubbery thing that had been jammed deep within her body. But ooh, the ritual wasn't complete.

With the rubbery thing still inside her, she watched her aunts leave, not saying a word to her. Aching to move her hands, she had been forced to watch as another woman, who simply identified herself as the Pleasure Mistress, proceeded to walk over to her and, without any inhibitions at all, start to suckle Rowena's nipples.

The shock of the act itself still mortified her. This, too, was not something women talked about. Later, she learned, it was the Pleasure Mistress' job to ensure that, after her woman's barrier had been breached, she could climax, thus making it easier for the fertile semen of the male to climb up inside her body and attach itself to her eager egg.

Whatever! Hence, after suckling her nipples, the Pleasure Mistress had moved the rubbery thing in and out of her wet channel. Then she had moved her lips to a small nub nestled within her crotch. One touch from the Pleasure Mistress' lips on her nub had caused her to climax. The shame of it was that she had climaxed not once, but twice.

If Rowena could have crawled anywhere, she would have. Instead, after her aunts came back in for a progress report, she had been bathed, perfumed and dressed. Now she was in the Supreme High Fertility Council chambers and about to be forced to pick a mate.

Then she would rut with him until he died. That was the blunt truth of it. No fertile man, once he had sex with a woman who was in the throes of the Maida curse, had yet to live for more than two days. Rowena sympathized with their plight.

Her sister and mother would say men didn't deserve their sympathy. After all, it was men who had started the wars that ravaged their homeland. It was men who let loose the first radioactive bombs and it was men who had created the fertility trap. The only thing was they had invented that trap for women, not vice versa, or so the myths went.

Rowena didn't care what anyone said. Being forced to rut with a woman when you knew it meant certain death couldn't whet any man's appetite, hence the use of the drugs. *Or just maybe the men don't know what happens to them.* That idea warranted more attention. She wondered if she could use that to her benefit, even as she vowed to find a cure.

It was her silent vow she made to herself. After all, if Maida women could organize themselves to find and generate food, care for the wounded, tend the sick and forge ahead after the last war, then surely she could devote her life to one crusade.

Rowena was suddenly jolted out of her daydream. Her heartbeat sped up as four men were paraded before her. For a moment, she forgot about her plight as their masculine scents wafted through her highly sensitive body. All four wore the traditional black robes, which covered them from head to ankle. Each had a small slit showcasing their eyes and they were barefoot. One man wore an ankle bracelet, a trinket no doubt from a woman, as no Maida men were allowed to own anything of value.

Of all the men, one stood out. He was at least two heads taller than the other three, yet he kept his head down. It wasn't a submissive pose. She liked the way he had a wide stance, as if he were getting ready to run. She noted his feet, like all the men's, were heavily hennaed. The designs were said to help entice a woman. Truthfully, they were unnecessary.

Rowena knew once she picked one, they would have the privacy of a special bedchamber. It would be there that she would get the honor of seeing her mate's naked body. Her choice today, though, followed tradition. She had to choose simply by observing their mannerisms and by listening to their answers. She was allowed to ask each male one question. For each, it had to be a different question.

The first was brought forward. He all but bounced on the spot, reminding her of a playful cat. Her body didn't respond to his nearness at all. When he answered her question with a long, convoluted reply, she knew he was the type who liked to hear himself speak.

The second man was brought forward. Rowena didn't like him at all. He looked too delicate for her taste and dumb to boot, as she listened to his reply to her question.

When the third man was ushered forward, he didn't come willingly, which raised her interest. He all but dragged his feet. He kept his head down. She sensed it was a challenge for him. Clasping her hands behind her back, she approached him.

"He is?" she asked, speaking to the guard at his side.

"Identification number 7653," answered the female guard.

Rowena had to look up. "You may raise your head."

With casual grace, she watched as the man straightened. With his head held high, he towered over her, which almost alarmed her.

Tulon growled in frustration. The last thing he wanted to do was acknowledge the petite woman standing in front of him. However, her voice beckoned him. It wasn't loud, or crass...it was like the whistling wind, ruffling his senses. That he didn't like.

So he did what came naturally to his kind. He lifted his head and glared at her, forcing her to shy away. He knew he had succeeded. She took one small, elegant step back. *Not enough.* Then he was forced to look at her.

Hair the color of chestnuts was cut short, cropped to frame her features. There was a curl to her hair she fought. He watched her tuck a stray piece behind her right ear. Oval, light blue eyes, high cheekbones and a long slender neck framed a tiny body. She only reached his chest, even wearing the high-heeled black boots she had forced her feet into. She looked none too comfortable in them was his first impression, as she attempted another step back and almost stumbled.

Her breasts, however, were an entirely different thing. The red gauzelike dress she wore that reached from her neck to her knees did nothing to deter his gaze. After all, he supposed, that was the purpose of the sin-like material. Enough to tantalize the eye, make the mind work and the body sweat. Enough to whet his appetite. Instantly he hated her.

What shook him the most was her scent. *She smells like that blasted lush, green meadow—clean and crisp. And worse, a woman in heat.*

The memory of that green ripe meadow soared into his mind. He recalled the acute feeling of hunger, the likes of which he had never experienced before, and how it gnawed at him. His body had ached to feel the grass caress his skin. The meadow smelled clean and crisp, filled with new growth.

After eating his fill, his senses, lost in the ecstasy and newness of the moment, had gone blind. His only saving grace after the hunting party managed to capture him was he had been in human form. They thought the stallion they had been chasing had vanished back into the Dark Forest. They never once made the connection that man and beast were one. He had hoped they would search the forest, but alas, as he found out later, a naked male in his prime was too good to go to waste.

The woman took a step toward him. Her sweet, musky, womanly cream assaulted his senses and he was powerless to stop his nostrils from flaring, trying to suck as much of her scent as possible into his body. He wanted to eat her alive!

Instead he clenched his fists that were held ramrod straight at his side. What was he doing here? What was this place? And more importantly, who was this petite woman who was doing her best to intimidate him, not that it was succeeding. He almost laughed at her antics.

Hands on her hips, she tilted her head up at him and asked him the most benign question. He frowned. *Is this part of some weird game?*

"What matters to you most?" she asked.

Stupid woman. What mattered to all of his kind—freedom.

His eyes narrowed in disgust. When he didn't immediately answer, she had the audacity to quirk her neat little eyebrows at him, as if he were brain-dead.

"What matters to you most, 7653?" she repeated, her voice brushing like a warm summer's breeze deep into the recesses of his mind.

The use of that number as if it were a name made him want to snort in frustration. "Freedom," he snapped, looking her straight in the eye, willing her to understand.

A smile lit up his face when she retreated back a step. His senses also told him her heart had accelerated. *She, too, isn't immune to my voice.* For once, that gave him a smug sense of male satisfaction.

"Him," she said, turning her face to a woman standing at her side. Tulon knew she had to be of importance. She looked regal.

"Choose another," the woman replied, trying to usher the fourth male forward.

He fought the urge to glare at her. He was chosen, and while he wasn't sure for what, he didn't like that she thought him beneath her. Contempt and disdain had filled her voice.

"I will not, Mother. I choose him," said the spitfire with grim determination as her eyes turned to challenge her mother.

Mother! That was her mother who stood next to her, dressed like a matriarch. That would make the spitfire a what? *A princess...high priestess...whatever*. Tulon knew the game he had been forced to play just had its stakes raised.

What he had been chosen for had to be pretty special. He almost smiled as the mother of the spitfire nodded her acquiescence to her daughter.

When the petite woman kneeled in front of him, he fought the urge to lean down and pick her up. Realizing this must be part of their barbaric ceremony, he stood straighter.

"I take the 7653 to be my mate...your seed to my seed...let life quicken within me."

The words were barely audible as she mumbled them. An electric shock rippled through his body when she lightly kissed each of his toes. He could have stumbled back from that intimacy, but he forced the creature he was to endure. Sadly, he liked it too much.

That's it! He was then hauled away. No questions asked. No answers. Once in the hall, the fair-haired one who had stood next to him sneered at him.

"Lucky bastard. Enjoy the *rut* of your life," he said, as he was whisked away.

When the other two fair-haired men were taken to a different hall and he was left alone with only one female guard watching him, he thought about running.

But to where? He had no idea where he was. He had been blindfolded for the entire journey to this place. Once here, he had been bathed, his body hennaed and then ushered into the lineup. Breaking his code of silence, he asked the guard, "What was all that about?"

It took her a moment to realize he was asking something of importance. He noticed her pupils dilate in sexual awareness. He mentally cursed at himself. *How I hate what my voice does to the women of this place.* He wanted to shake sense into her. For once in his life, he wanted a straight answer.

He turned, as a voice behind him spoke, fully aware of who stood there—the mother.

"Pleasure my daughter well. Do your job. Nothing more. Do you hear me?" she stated, not expecting him to answer as she strode past him.

Pleasure her daughter well. It took a moment for that notion to be fully digested by him. *So that's what I was chosen for. Bed sport!* His nostrils flared at the insult, even as his body hummed its own eager answer. Blast his cock, which now stood at attention, lusting at the vision of ramming the petite woman into submission.

Chapter Four

Rowena wanted to hide or run. Ushered into the room, she kept her head down. She was dressed in the ceremonial sheer ankle-length dress, slit up the middle all the way to her belly button and only held together with two small pearl buttons past her breasts. She fought the urge to clutch what little material there was and bunch it around her body.

She tried hard not to look at the man, who was naked now. That thought brought a rush of heat to spread throughout her body. She wanted to reach down and clamp her legs shut, anything to stop the steady pulse that throbbed deep within her. The ache was becoming unbearable. Her pussy was drenched with cream. Her labia were swollen with a hungry need for the man's cock to be wedged deep within her aching core. Turning away from the large, plush bed that took up most of the chamber, she crossed the floor and moved as far as possible away from the man who, like her, was all but panting with lust.

Rowena knew she didn't need the pheromone injection. Her body had become wet simply by looking at specimen 7653. Now, however, she felt as if she were drowning in desire. Her breasts felt achy, heavy with need. Her body tingled with awareness as his fresh, clean, all-too-male scent caught her senses. Her pussy muscles clenched in anticipation of what they thought was to come.

She felt a steady beat between her legs. Her pussy was trying on its own to beckon the man closer—eagerly wanting the feel of him wedged deep within her.

She shook her head, once again hating her race's predicament. If she gave in to what her body craved and rutted the man senseless, then she was no better than the lowest of scum that made up the bottom of society. While all of her aunts and her mother told her it was her duty and that she didn't have a choice, she knew better.

Many said Maida civilization had entered the Enlightened Age. *How enlightened is this?* The idea of what she had to do was as barbaric to her as murdering a person with her own two hands. *Heck, I don't even need hands. I just need his cock and his seed—talk about a killer recipe.*

While their technological advances included the new skater-cruisers, which carried up to two people and hovered above the ground moving from colony to colony, Rowena thought they had yet to make the most important scientific discovery. Stopping the Maida curse was paramount.

After the war, women created the four colonies for the production of food and the advancement of scientific discoveries. Women lived within the colonies with large extended female families. All male children were raised in orphanages.

Each colony consisted of one large four-story round central building, which housed key scientists who oversaw specific technology geared to that colony. The First Colony catered to automation. The new aqua-fired terminals that kept all the colonies linked to each other were paramount to their future success.

The Second Colony was an art and manufacturing base and oversaw new fashion designs, including the new ultra-light fire-resistant lab coat Rowena usually wore. Their mandate combined art with purpose. Rowena highly doubted they had anything to do with the sheer ceremonial gown she had been forced to wear. *Then again, if the purpose is to leave as little to the imagination as possible, then I guess they succeeded.*

The Third Colony housed all the intellectuals who spent most of their time working on new legislation that was supposed to streamline thought-provoking literature. *As if?*

The Fourth Colony was the nuts and bolts of Maida. Most of the male laborers lived there. Only a handful were assigned to the other three colonies on a need basis. This colony oversaw all food production and the assembly of food supplies to the other three colonies.

Rowena sighed. While all the horrible scars of the war had been plowed under to be replaced with neat, tidy structures and pathways lined with manicured lawns, there was one scar that still hadn't healed.

Rowena was one of many Maida scientists across her world who worked long hours to find a cure for the sterility that still haunted her race. While none of the results showed promise, they, like she, would not give up.

She shivered with a strange longing as the man approached her. She knew her aunts would tell her it was Maida's destiny and her future that were at stake.

It's him or me. Both choices suck. She sensed his hesitation as he neared her body. She didn't need to turn. She knew he stood within arm's reach of her. For once in her life, she didn't know what to do. Give in to the need, the craving and her desires and all for what. Loud and clear in her mind was that dreaded word she had grown up hearing over and over again—procreation.

Blast the lot of them. She wiped away the tears that had traveled unchecked down her cheek. *Being a fertile woman sucks, big time.* She hated the cascade of emotions running through her body as much as she hated the man who stood a foot behind her.

Tulon knew he was drooling. Who wouldn't? The filly was in reach and in heat. While he sensed a part of her was eager, another stronger part was terrified. That emotion was loud and clear as she tried her best to avoid looking at him. She had moved to the farthest corner of the room. She was a blasted innocent. He cringed with that knowledge. It wasn't what his body wanted. It wasn't what his cock ached for.

He didn't want to be gentle, kind and loving at the moment. He ached to ram his shaft deep within her creamy cunt. He wanted to pound his cock into her tight entrance to satisfy his insatiable hunger. His stones were swollen with need and his blasted cock throbbed, seeking release. He was tempted to take matters into his own hands, but he knew it wouldn't be enough. Especially after scenting the filly's musky need.

These Maida people are strange. His kind would never resort to such an uncivilized practice. Mating was a dance. It had its own rhythm, its own season, and its own time. Plus there was the chase.

He fondly recalled the first time he had undertaken the perilous wild run through his lands to catch the eye of a mare in heat. It had been exhilarating. And the reward was sweet. So deliciously rich that recalling it now only caused his shaft to thicken more.

Sweat formed on his brow as his body anticipated what was to come. Tulon took a calming breath. The last thing he wanted to do was act like a *youngling*—so eager he spilled his seed before claiming the prize.

Tulon cursed silently. He sensed it was this filly's time and her need was great. While he didn't relish the job he had been picked for, his cock certainly had his attention. His stones ached with heavy need. The minute she had walked into the room, he knew he was doomed.

Who would have thought that Maida clothing could be made to look sexy? Heck, for the past two years he had only seen the females wearing khaki uniforms. This was an entirely new sight for his tired eyes. Long legs, thank the Saints. He had always liked a filly who could run. Small feet, a firm solid ass narrowed to a tiny waist, but her breasts, now those were something his hands would enjoy.

He knew she was shy as she tried without success to wrap herself tighter in the sheer material. He also knew she was avoiding looking at him. He wasn't wearing a stitch of clothing, but he wasn't cold. His body had been bathed again and oiled. He had recognized the scent of the oil as it had been lathered all over, and he meant *all over*, his body.

The oil originated from the tempra plant, known to his kind for its aphrodisiac qualities. It surprised him that these people would harvest such a plant. He had thought the exotic plant only grew on his lands.

From what he had come to know of the Maida they would never venture into the Dark Forest.

He knew the scent of the oil was permeating his cells. The plant heightened one's sexual awareness. *Like I need that now.* He could have laughed at that, but knew better. This was not the time for laughter. This was the time for him to take control.

Like any good stallion, he knew this mare needed to be herded to her own body's desires and that challenged him. He knew exactly what she needed, even if she didn't. So he moved forward. He let her sense him behind her. Still she didn't move. *Well, so be it.*

With courage and lust that would have made any Centaur proud, he strode forward, wrapped his arms around her and with no preamble placed a hand on her front mound. He had staked his claim. Made his move and now he waited. After the shock of his brazen act had settled into her body, he leaned into her, letting her get a good feel of his rock-hard shaft that rubbed against her backside with need. Then he spread his fingers wider so they could rub her thatch of pubic hair through the sheer dress. She moaned deeply. The sound fired itself from his toes to his cock.

"Get away from me," she said, attempting to buck him away.

He smiled. This he could deal with. Heck, her firm ass up tight against him made his cock pulse with hunger.

Towering over her, he pushed her forward, forcing her to brace her body with her arms on the wall.

Again she bucked away, unaware what the movement did to him. He could have grinned more but passion blazed behind his eyes as he forced himself to the task at hand. Why she fought him remained a mystery to him. *Heck, she picked me. What, is she having cold feet or something?*

"Woman, you picked me. I'm just doing what I was assigned to do. And trust me, I do it well." He drawled on the last part, letting her envision the double meaning of that statement.

"Get away from me!" she snapped, trying to wriggle out from his tight hold.

With one hand holding her mound fast, he gently moved his other hand to let his fingers slip inside her dress—letting her know what he was capable of. "I don't think so," he replied, as a finger dipped down the crease of her swollen cleft while his breath teased the curls that were now in disarray around her ear.

"Brute! You don't understand. If I do this, then you die." She turned to face him.

Tulon laughed. *That's a good one.* Trust a Maida woman to come up with that weird logic. He laughed even louder.

He let her push him aside, giving her the space she needed. Bright blue eyes that reminded him of a cloudless day glared at him in fury.

"You don't understand," she said, wearily.

Now this Tulon liked. His shaft bobbing close to her belly. He took his rigid cock in his hand and rubbed the glistening tip of it over her silky smooth stomach. She stilled.

He watched her tilt her head up to look at him.

"Okay, let me explain this."

Tulon knew passion when he saw it. Her eyes glistened with it. He could smell her wet, creamy desire for sex opening her throbbing pussy more. Even while she was willing him to listen to her, her hand had unconsciously moved to touch his chest. He knew she was completely unaware of her actions. But he wasn't.

His cock bucked in reply. Through the sheer fabric, he saw her pebbled nipples. With his teeth, he bent down and unclasped the two tiny buttons. Then he licked first one and then the other nipple. Thankfully she stopped talking.

Rowena was in a living nightmare. Her body was on fire with a need that was practically burning her alive. Her senses were chaotic, spiraling out of control. The mating fever was racing through her system and she could have killed her aunts for giving her that blasted injection.

"You don't understand. This isn't me. I'm not usually like this. They injected me with hormones to overstimulate me," she said, breathlessly. It was then she noticed her hand was tracing the light dusting of dark hairs that covered his chest.

"Augh!" She pushed at him, attempting to scramble farther away from him.

"Let me remind you. You picked me. This wasn't my choice," said the man.

His voice was a deep rumble that vibrated through her body straight down to her already wet, pulsing core.

Oh, by the Saints, his voice. Did he have to speak? She shook her head, trying to clear her cloudy thoughts. Simply listening to his voice dazed her. It made her think of wild sex, tangled limbs and uncontrolled desires. For one moment, she contemplated slapping herself—hoping pain would lessen the desire.

"Sit!" she screeched. She was amazed when he didn't object. She sensed he wasn't a man who liked to take orders from women. Her mother had told her all about those men. That was why they were chosen for the labor camps. They couldn't be trusted. If the men were to group together and use their puny brains for a change, they could do a lot of damage.

Maida women would never let men attempt to control their lives again. However, why she had picked him was clear. He was man to the core. He was so male, he scared—no, thrilled—her. So she told herself, moving yet again to the furthest corner of the room.

"Please don't talk. Let me explain this to you. I'm a scientist. I've been trying for years now to work out a cure for this illness, but so far no luck." She paused and shook her head when he almost opened his mouth.

Rowena knew hearing that rumbling, baritone voice again would cause her body to melt. She would, in all likelihood, crawl to the blasted man on her knees and beg him to plunge his magnificent cock right into her pulsing pussy right there on the hard ceramic floor. That erotic thought caused her to shiver.

Quickly continuing on, she played with the bunch of material she had fisted into her hands. Anything to keep her anchored to one spot. "A century ago, after the last war, Maida women came to realize that the radioactive fallout caused many of us to become sterile. Only a handful of men and women are fertile. It's a mixed blessing. Fertile women are cursed. If we don't mate within a given timeframe, our minds begin to break down on the molecular level. We quite literally go crazy.

"Once we mate, the disease inherent in our makeup gets passed to the male. Within days, if that, they die. Do you understand me? If I rut with you...okay, if I fuck you...in all likelihood, you will die tomorrow. So, I can't. I'm asking you to leave. Escape. Do whatever you can to get away from me."

Rowena gulped as she tugged forcibly on the sheer material.

"I know this place inside out. I can help you escape, but it has to be now. Next door there's a hidden tunnel that travels through the walls of this complex. I discovered it years ago. If the door is unlocked, I can get you to that tunnel and then you simply follow it to the end. At the end is an iron grate. I made sure this morning the grate was unlocked. Once you open that grate, go two klicks, then there is a large meadow and after that there's the Dark Forest. I don't normally tell people to enter the forest, but if you stay close to the edges you should be all right and I know Maida guards won't enter the forest..."

"Let's go now," said the man, who had moved so fast Rowena almost stumbled.

One minute he was sitting on the bed, intently listening to her plea while holding his rod in his hand and the next thing she knew he was standing directly in front of her. She had to blink a couple of times to clear the rush of sexual desire that channeled through her system.

She moved to the door, thanking the Saints he didn't say anything more. She listened, hoping no one was on the other side. For all she knew, there could be a large audience and the minute she opened the door they would applaud. After all she had been put through today, that wouldn't have shocked or surprised her. Thankfully, when she gingerly opened it to peek down the long corridor, no one was within sight.

Briskly walking to the adjacent room, she turned the doorknob. Nothing. *Blast it, it's locked.* She could have wept as all her hope dissipated. They were stuck. There was nothing she could do now.

When the man elbowed her out of the way, she meekly moved aside, wondering what he planned to do. She watched as he turned the knob. When he, too, realized it was locked, he simply pushed her farther to the side and then, horrified, she watched as he rammed the door down with his own body. The blatant display of male strength, combined with the sense of danger and mystery, enflamed her sexual need.

The shrill sound of a siren broke her thoughts.

When the man grabbed her arm and yanked her into the room she felt affronted. Having never been manhandled before, she didn't like it one bit, knowing that was yet another lie. Where his hand had grasped her she tingled. Her body felt electrified with a needy heat.

"Where is the tunnel?" he demanded, turning her to face him.

Rowena let him shake her. His blasted voice snaked its way straight to her hot pussy, which was dripping with need. She hated him even more for that.

Motioning to the far right-hand corner in the room, she watched as his fingers moved along the wall. When he found the outline of the tunnel, he pushed against it. Once again, like the door, it opened to his brute strength.

Rowena heard the guards running down the corridor. She planned to stall them for as long as she could. She felt relief in knowing she had set the man free, even at her own expense. *So be it.*

When the man once again yanked her arm, she fought him.

"I'm staying. I gave you your freedom. So run." She hissed at him while trying to drag her arm away.

"You're coming with me," he commanded.

Mortified, Rowena struggled against him. He simply picked her up like she was a child and hauled her into the tunnel with him. Thankful that the tunnel was built as high as the large cathedral-like ceilings of the building, she twisted and turned, attempting to get him to put her down.

"I'm saving you," he said, smacking her ass.

The stimulation of that stopped her cold. No one had ever dared to do that to her before. The heat of his slap singed her deeply, leaving her body scorching for more. Worse, he kept his hand over her ass. Too afraid to speak for fear of moaning loudly, which would only inform him how much her body had enjoyed his smack, she shut up.

Her head continued to bob up and down as the man ran with her like she was a sack of food through the tunnel to freedom. The view of his naked ass muscles bunching as he ran caused her to shiver. Who knew watching a man run naked could be so erotic?

None of this was what she had been expecting. The man's actions hadn't been what she predicted. There was something about him that stirred a strange, almost terrifying feeling within the pit of her stomach.

Hoping her reaction to him was due to her elevated hormones, she bit her lip to keep from moaning with need as his male spicy scent cascaded straight through her body, causing her breasts to tighten and tingle.

Chapter Five

Ahead, like the woman had said, was the grate. With one shove from his hand, the heavy black metal moved out of the way. *Freedom*! Tulon couldn't believe his luck. *The Saints are with me today.*

He knew the feisty filly was silent for a reason. After smacking her ass, his nostrils had flared. She was aroused like never before. *Who would have thought*? The urge to give her round, solid ass another playful smack snuck up on him. This time she couldn't contain her moan of pleasure. It pleased him to know that as innocent as she was, she was a wild one. Once mated, this filly would enjoy a good ride. His cock once again jumped to attention with his own need.

"Put me down," she demanded.

Tulon noted how breathless she sounded. He would like nothing better than to put her down. It was hard holding her over his shoulder—she squirmed like a slippery tick.

"Settle down. We'll soon be at the Dark Forest," he said, never once slowing down. Tulon could smell the meadow now. After that was the forest. Then his freedom. And only then would he let the woman go. Or better yet, give in to the need she had for him.

He hadn't been about to enlighten her that he wasn't Maida after realizing her plight. His kind were sheltered from her people thanks to their old magic. They were unaffected by the puny skirmishes of the Maida or the other humanoids who lived on Alvaron.

Centaurs had existed since the beginning of time. They were made up of old foundation magic, which had created Alvaron. While it was true they were now confined to their own lands, it had been necessary. Once, as legend had it, they had befriended the people. Then the people had tried to tame them, tried to corral them to their own needs. Centaurs were not to be tamed. So the peace-loving creatures of his kind had simply vanished from existence a millennium ago, or so people believed.

They became a thing of legend and myth. It was simpler that way. Armed now with more knowledge of the Maida, he knew that to be true like never before. However, he wasn't blind to the woman's plight. He planned to discover if she spoke the truth. Then, judging her need, he might be tempted to help. He relished the idea of getting release. Her scent was driving him crazy. The tip of his cock was wet, like he was a *youngling*. She infuriated him.

"Put me down. I can't go into the Dark Forest." She once again tried to squirm out of his tight hold.

"Shut up," he demanded, tempted to give her ass another solid smack. However she wasn't the only one affected by her hormones and now was not the time to add fuel to the fire.

His sensitive hearing could detect runners—in all likelihood warriors. And if they were anything like the heathen lot that had initially captured him, they would be armed with flying nets. Those he couldn't outrun. Picking up the pace, he moved the woman onto his other shoulder. Spying the meadow, he didn't slow, even though his body craved to reach down and brush the tall stalks of fresh, green grass. Instead, he dove for the cover of the forest, letting the darkness engulf them.

The woman immediately fell silent. *Smart, for once.* She ceased her squirming and settled onto his shoulder. Even though it was quite dark, it didn't slow Tulon down. As a Centaur, his eyesight was supreme. Casually, he moved around the living trees, willing them as before to grant his way. They sensed what he was and didn't hesitate. That, too, was a blessing. He knew the Madia woman had no idea of the real dangers lurking in the woods.

Judging he was safe from the warriors, he finally put the squirming woman down. She landed hard on a tree stump. Then he stalked off to take care of some urgent business. What he wanted to do was ram his cock deep inside the feisty spitfire whose body was imprinted on his brain. And her ass—it was no surprise clutching onto it for the better part of an hour had caused his shaft to bulge even more.

Tulon growled in frustration. As much as he hated it, he knew the blasted pheromone injection they had given him wasn't the only reason he was forced to ease the ache in his cock. He felt like a bloody *youngling* around her. It made him mad.

He hoped anger would ease the need, but it didn't. If anything the vision of ramming her hot and heavy, of plunging into her tight, wet opening made him almost spill his seed before he made it around the large tree trunk. *The last thing I need is an audience.* He groaned. Forced to take matters into his own hands infuriated him on a level he had never experienced before.

Where did he go? Thankful to no longer be jostled about, she smarted from being dumped onto a tree stump. He had stalked off without a word. Her eyes had long ago adjusted to the dusk-like darkness in the forest.

The trees were immense both in width and height. She had heard rumors about the Dark Forest, but the fear those stories wrought had kept the scientist she was from daring the impossible. Not so anymore.

She couldn't help but gawk. Vegetation the likes of which she had never seen before vied for her eyes. But it was the towering, thick trees that captivated her. Then a small groan caused her to still.

She scampered off the tall stump to seek out the man as curiosity got the better of her. *He could be hurt. Maybe he pulled a muscle from carrying me like feedstock. Serves him right.* His groans didn't sound pleasant. However, when she came within view, her steps faltered.

He was a sight to behold. His long jet-black hair fell in disarray down his back, his head was thrown back and in his hand was his long, very hard, magnificent cock. Mesmerized by the erotic sight and with her heart accelerating to a feverish pitch, she watched.

Immediately she felt a pool of cream congeal between her thighs. As much as Rowena wanted to move, she couldn't. In his hand he held his cock, and up and down he stroked it, pumped it even, at a furious pace that caused her to wet her lips. Without realizing it she edged closer. She had to see more. She ached for more.

"Go!" he commanded. His eyes were squeezed shut as he concentrated on the task at hand.

"No," she replied, cautiously approaching him so she stood within arm's reach. A longing to touch, caress and stroke him overtook her thoughts. With boldness she didn't know she possessed, she moved even closer. He was gloriously naked as when he had first entered the room. Now however, here amidst the sanctity of the forest, he was in his element. He looked like an untamed man whose body was made for rutting.

When he didn't respond anymore, she moved her hand over his. *I have to do this. It's all my fault.* The man's need for her had been heightened by the injection and this was his way of dealing with it. While the idea should have appalled her, it did the opposite.

Rowena was not going to fool herself. She'd love to have his cock, the one in her hand, wedged tight within her slick throbbing pussy. To do so would sentence this man to death and as much as she was sexually frustrated at the moment, she couldn't do it—even knowing her sanity wouldn't last much longer.

"Am I doing it right?" she asked, watching his facial expression for clues.

"Yes," he groaned.

Then he turned his head to look at her. Chocolate brown eyes of mystery watched her work him. It was intoxicating. Her hand was now slick with his need as she pumped him.

"Faster," he moaned, placing his hand over hers to pick up the pace.

His shaft was elegantly long and thick. She was surprised when it bulged even more. Then he arched his head and groaned loudly as he came in her hand. He was sticky warm and his masculine musky, wild scent raced straight to every cell in her eager body.

She licked her hand, needing to taste his seed. He tasted salty, and there was a hint of wildness in his semen that made her want to rub it all over her aching nipples. *Where did that thought come from?* A blush stole over her features, adding to her heat.

"Thank you," he growled, moving away from her.

Rowena was disappointed. She wasn't sure what to expect, but his swift rejection told her she wasn't skilled in the art of lovemaking.

"You didn't need to do that."

His voice was a low rumble that cascaded straight to her, clenching core muscles. *By the Saints, if only he knew what his voice did to me.*

Moving to where he sat on a large stump, she answered. "I got you into this mess. It was the least I could do. I know what that injection does to your body and, well, that was my way of helping. I hope."

She longed to lick her palm to taste his essence again, yet he was watching her with such a haunted, confused look on his face, she didn't dare. Too bad, because she had really liked the salty, untamed taste of him. *Then again, maybe it's a good thing I can't. The last thing I need is to become addicted to the flavor of him. I'd rather eat dead leaves.* Anything to keep her scientific mind working while her body betrayed her real cravings.

Tulon couldn't believe it. The woman thought he had to take care of his need because of some stupid injection. Did she have no idea how truly exotic she looked, clad in the sheer dress that left little to the imagination? The fact that she was barefoot was an added torture. Her small, delicate feet intrigued him. He would like nothing better than to lick and suck on each one of her tiny toes.

Spilling his seed did take some of the edge off him, but he knew it wasn't enough. Nor would it last long. What he ached to do was slowly plunge into her swollen cunt until she climaxed again and again from his pleasuring her. He was also mortified she felt responsible for his agitated state. *Well, she is, but it has to do with her luscious body and not the needle.*

"Come here," he commanded, deciding it was time he eased a bit of her ache. He smelled her flowery womanly cream and it beckoned him. He wanted to taste her. No, he needed to lap at her nectar that was driving all of his senses nuts until she was dry and well satisfied.

When she didn't move, he repeated his statement. "Come here." He patted the spot beside his lap.

"Just what do you plan to do?" she asked.

Tulon liked how the filly balked at getting closer to him, even as she tentatively approached. Her sexual need was so great, it practically shimmered her skin. His eyes could see the wet evidence of her cream coating the insides of her thighs and he growled in approval.

"Sit," he demanded, grabbing her arms and forcing her to straddle his lap. The feel of her sheer gown on his leg hairs caused his cock to jump to life again.

"We can't—"

"Stop talking and for once listen to the wind." He ran a hand calmly up and down her back.

"What does the wind have to do with...ooh, that feels so good," she said, accepting his touch.

Thankfully, she stopped talking.

Tulon liked how she arched her back, inviting his touch—all the while providing him with a better view of those luscious breasts of hers. Again he stroked her, letting her get used to the feel of his hands on her, needing her to accept the pulse of excitement as his cock grew painfully rigid nestled between her splayed legs.

Her body was smooth like the warm green grass and she smelled like oranges and lemons, causing him to salivate. Small moans of pleasure from her egged him on. As innocent as she was, he knew she ached for more.

Moving his hands to her thighs, he worked his way up both silky legs. Long legs. Legs he would love to have wrapped around him as he plunged himself deep inside her heat.

She stilled. Fear danced to life inside her eyes.

"Shh, it will be okay, relax," he ordered. He seductively lowered his voice, knowing it would soothe her.

Without preamble, he snaked his hand closer to her achy core and then, before she could protest, he slid a finger down her wet clit.

Her body shuddered with intense need. She was dripping with sex. Her pussy was so hot, it beckoned to him like fresh grass. He noticed her sky-blue eyes were wide open, but for once her lips were closed shut. She wasn't objecting to his ministrations. For that he was thankful.

"Lean back and spread your legs wider. I'm going to play with that warm pussy of yours" he commanded, all the while sliding a finger back and forth over her wet opening—teasing her clit into submission.

When she did as instructed, he gave in to the need to feel her breasts. There was only one small button clasping her dress together. With one nip, they were gone. Two milky white breasts spilled forth and gleamed at him. They were a treasure. He flicked a tongue over first one nipple then another. She moaned in response. Then he closed his mouth over her sun-dipped buds and suckled. His cock thickened even more.

"May I?" she asked, inching her hand around to grasp his throbbing cock.

"No," he growled, with more force than he intended. Truth was, he knew if she put her petite hands on his shaft again, the creature he was would reign supreme and in no time at all she'd be on all fours with his cock ramming her like there was no tomorrow.

"Let me pleasure you, please," he added, moving to suckle her other breast. Her body had been lubricated with the tempra plant too, and the wild taste of it on her skin enhanced all of his senses.

"Tulon," he said, sliding a finger deep into her wet opening.

"What?" she rasped out, her breathing shallow as she fought not to squirm with need.

"My name is Tulon," he said again, slowly withdrawing his finger, only to plunge it back in faster and faster to stroke her clutching pussy muscles.

"Ooh."

He loved the sound of her moans. Her head was thrown back and her eyes were closed as she let his finger work her creamy core. "My name's Rowena."

"That has a nice sound to it. Do you like this?" he asked, knowing full well she did.

"Stop talking," she commanded.

Tulon couldn't help but chuckle. Her body was strung as tight as an archer's bow.

"Is something funny?" she asked.

The last thing Tulon wanted was for her to start reasoning a way out of the pleasure he was giving her. He simply wanted her to enjoy it for all it was worth. It was the least he could do. After all, if she felt this good with her hot pussy clutching at his finger then he knew sooner rather than later his cock would find a home deep inside her.

For now, though, he wanted her to climax on him, with his finger wedged tight inside her. Moving her slick folds open more, he let the forest's breath wash over it. Her nub of pleasure pebbled to life. He rolled it with his thumb, all the while stroking two fingers inside her while his mouth devoured her breasts. When she came, it was hard. He let her grind her hips into him as she fought the cliff, but he wanted her to leap over it. Pebbling her nub harder, he used the power of his voice.

"Come for me, Rowena, you can do it. That's it. Let it happen," he said, loving the moment when she arched her back, threw back her head and came. His two fingers felt her pussy muscles milk him. Then she slumped forward. Soothingly he pulled his fingers out and licked them, loving the womanly, flowery taste of her.

"I can't believe I just let you do that to me," she said, pushing off him somewhat as she attempted to reassert her control.

I don't think so, thought Tulon.

"What I'd really like to do is lie you down in a meadow, spread your legs and then stuff my cock so deep inside you, then you'll know what it feels like to be truly fucked. How's that?" said Tulon, grinning with macho pride as a flush of heat stole over her features.

"I don't think that's a good idea," she said, attempting to clasp her dress together to hide her breasts from his eyes.

"Sounds good to me," said a baritone voice that originated from over Tulon's shoulder.

Immediately Tulon stood, placing Rowena behind him.

"Who's there?" he asked, his body poised to run or fight, if need be.

Tulon watched as ten men strode out of the forest's brush. He didn't like the look of them.

"Are you sure?" said one man to another.

Tulon assumed the man with the crown of twigs on his head was the leader. He was an imposing sight. As tall as Tulon, he was broad of shoulder and looked capable of killing a person with his large trunk-like hands.

"I'm not completely sure, but he's got the same scent as the stallion we had been tracking," squeaked the man into the leader's ears.

"But he's not a stallion. He's a man."

"A well-endowed man and he will do," said a husky woman's voice as she, too, materialized from the blanket of trees.

"Lady MacQuellion," whispered Rowena, bowing low to the woman who strode forward with ease.

"You know her?" hissed Tulon, not liking that he wasn't in the know.

"Only in myth. I didn't think she was real. But she's exactly how the myths portray her." Awe filled Rowena's voice.

"Is she friendly in those myths of yours?" asked Tulon, hoping the answer was yes. He had a sneaking suspicion it wasn't.

Before Rowena could answer him, the lady moved forward. She was clad in a fawn-colored dress that reached her knees. The material attempted to conceal her well-endowed breasts, but it didn't succeed. Strapped to her back was a familiar sight to his eyes. She carried a bow and arrows and, by the look of her muscular arms, she knew how to use them. Also strapped to her thigh was the hint of a knife. She was well armed for a lady of ranking. Tulon knew that the men accompanying her would be even better armed. Things were looking worse by the moment.

"Good to know someone knows who I am and you too may bow to me," she said, pointing her finger at Tulon.

"I bow to no one," he replied curtly.

Immediately two of her guards had him by his arms before he could move. He forced himself to still as she came forward.

"He does smell like that stallion...could it be?" She boldly eyed him. "It doesn't matter, he will do. We need fresh seed and I, for one, have need of him. He's well hung," she declared, motioning to her guards to tie him up.

"Run, Rowena," said Tulon.

"Oh, she's coming with us." Lady MacQuellion motioned for the guards and, in a blink, Rowena's hands were tied together.

"What do you want with us?" asked Tulon, not liking the sly looks the men in the group gave him. They weren't friendly looks and it caused the hairs on the back of his neck to stand on end.

"You will see. Our need of you is great," she chimed, ushering them through the forest canopy.

The men's evil cackles didn't appease the anxious feeling in the pit of Tulon's stomach one bit. And he didn't like their crude gesturing toward his shaft, which was still standing at attention, all thanks to the taste of Rowena.

Chapter Six

Rowena couldn't believe her eyes. *Lady MacQuellion is supposed to be a myth, not a real person. And the men, are they truly Tree Wraiths?* It seemed hard to imagine. But no one had ever ventured into the Dark Forest. Maybe the myths were real.

If so, what did the Lady want with her and Tulon? Listening to the Lady's frank talk, she knew exactly what she wanted with Tulon. She bristled at the idea. She realized she had no hold over him and told herself it didn't matter.

"Place her in that hut," said Lady MacQuellion, indicating a small, derelict thatched round dwelling on the far side of the village.

"You, come with me." She motioned the guards to bring Tulon to the large hut in the middle of the village.

Fear clawed through Rowena. She didn't want to be separated from him. It terrified her. *Just when did he become my anchor?*

"Tulon," choked Rowena, too afraid to give voice to her fear.

"I will come willingly, if she comes with me," said Tulon.

Rowena could have wept for joy. Even in all the uncertainty, he stood tall, regally proud before Lady MacQuellion, stating his demands.

"Fine, suit yourself. Bring her," snapped the Lady.

And once again Rowena found herself standing next to Tulon as they moved to the center of the hut. She breathed a sigh of relief at being near him. Why she felt comforted and safe with him, even though they had been taken prisoner, baffled her common no-nonsense mind. Then it dawned on her, she was starting to lose her reasoning. If she didn't succumb to the sexual need for fulfillment that was a raw itch burning under her highly sensitive skin, she'd soon go crazy.

"Daughter, I have brought you a gift," said Lady MacQuellion to a young woman huddled next to a large stone hearth.

Beside the stone hearth, centered in the middle of the hut, were pallets and on top of them animal furs.

"I don't want him. I want the stallion," muttered the strange woman, who hadn't bothered to acknowledge their presence.

"I told you before there is no stallion. There never was. But my dear, the man is well..."

"Well what, Mother?" asked the young woman, turning angry green eyes at her mother when she finally looked at Rowena and Tulon.

"He is well equipped to deal with your needs."

"I highly doubt that," she mumbled, slowly standing up from the hearth.

The young woman walked forward. Her only covering was a black bear fur draped across her body that she clutched with one hand. Rowena highly doubted she wore clothing underneath it.

Then it dawned on Rowena what was happening. Tulon was about to become a sacrifice. If the legends were true, and so far they appeared to be, this woman needed to mate with Tulon to produce a male heir, who would then be handed over to the Tree Wraiths. Once he rutted with this woman, his blood would then be spilled and sprinkled over the forest floor as an offering to the Forest Saints.

Rowena tried to warn Tulon, but she was silenced by a cold look from Lady MacQuellion.

In eerie fascination, she watched as the young lady grasped Tulon's shaft. Within a second, it grew to life. Rowena narrowed her eyes in frustration, hating that he had responded to this unknown woman's touch. Shocked, she watched as the woman stroked it, causing it to thicken. Tulon bounced on the balls of his feet and she knew he was trying hard to stifle the desire, but it wasn't doing any good.

"So, daughter, will he do?" asked Lady MacQuellion.

"Nicely," answered the young woman, wetting her lips and never once taking her eyes off Tulon's large shaft.

If anything had been within reach, Rowena knew she wouldn't have hesitated to smash it over the young woman who was salivating on the spot. Jealousy pooled thick and dark inside her. *Why isn't Tulon doing something to stop her?*

Maybe if she had something to use as a club, she'd bash Tulon's head in. She bit the inside of her mouth when the woman knelt down beside Tulon and took his engorged cock into her small, inviting mouth.

By the Saints, he'd gone to heaven and it was pure bliss. As much as he was enjoying the young woman's attention to his cock, Tulon wasn't stupid. Something wasn't entirely right with the picture. As much as the creature he was told him to shut up and simply enjoy the pleasure while it lasted, he couldn't. Plus, he knew Rowena was fuming. That he found highly amusing.

"While she's got my cock in her mouth, do you mind telling me what's going on?" asked Tulon, amazed he sounded pissed off while the young woman's tongue slipped expertly over all of his shaft's sensitive ridges.

"My daughter needs to mate and she's quite particular. She has chosen you," answered Lady MacQuellion, ushering the remaining guards out of the hut.

"Ahh, yes...but as much as I'd like to comply, we don't plan on staying," stated Tulon, forcing the young woman's head to move off his rigid cock. He was enjoying it too much. What he wanted was reasoning.

"That's right, we're not staying," said Rowena, attempting to back him up.

He could have smiled at that but didn't dare.

"She only needs you for one night. After that, you may leave," said Lady MacQuellion.

"And just who is she?" asked Tulon, hating that he didn't even know the name of the young woman who was obviously well versed in the art of pleasing a male.

"This is my daughter, Felicia. She is at her peak—"

"Mother!" admonished Felicia, quickly standing. With that one movement, the fur covering fell to the floor.

Tulon sucked in his breath. She was half-fawn. She was a Betikhan. Distant cousin to Centaurs. Her head was human, but the rest of her from her shoulders down was fawn. With the fur covering most of her body, he hadn't noticed that her two legs had deer hooves instead of feet or women's legs. He knew from Rowena's indrawn breath she was shocked. And worse, probably mortified.

"What are you?" asked Rowena.

"She is a Betikhan," answered Tulon, reaching down to grab the fur covering. Gently, he draped it around the young woman, whose blush of embarrassment colored her pale facial features.

"You know what she is?" asked Lady MacQuellion, clearly impressed.

"Yes, I do...but she's not your real daughter," stated Tulon.

"No, sadly I could have no daughters. I found her ten cycles ago and claimed her as my own. As of late, though, she's changed. She's grown wilder—"

"Mother, please—"

"Hush, child, if you want this man to help—"

"I don't. What I want is the stallion," she stated, turning her back to them once again to sit by the hearth.

"What stallion is she talking about?" asked Rowena.

"Two years ago, Felicia saw a stallion running wild through these woods. It was the first time she saw a four-legged. Ever since then, we've been hunting for it. She seems to think that the stallion might be able to help her find others of her kind. I am not so sure," sighed Lady MacQuellion.

"To be honest, she's not been herself of late. She is crazed with mating. She has mated with almost all of my Tree Wraiths. Don't look so shocked, she is a creature of the wild with magic running in her veins. I have only been trying to help," admonished Lady MacQuellion, moving to a large barrel that housed fresh water.

Tulon watched as she dished out a bowl of fresh water for them.

He was shocked. This creature had spied him two years ago when he had run wild through the woods. He tried recalling seeing her. He couldn't. She must have been well concealed. He hadn't even sensed another magical being. Then again, he'd had other things on his mind—namely, food.

"I don't follow this. What does mating have to do with helping her?" asked Rowena, interrupting Tulon's wild thoughts as she took the bowl of water from Lady MacQuellion.

"She's like you, Rowena. A Betikhan must mate or die. That is their existence. Like you, she is cursed," answered Tulon, turning to look Rowena in the eye.

"I believe you are right. Felicia is now aging at an accelerated rate. After she mates with one of my Tree Wraiths, her aging slows down, but it's only a temporary fix. She needs one of her kind. Unfortunately I found her far on the other side of the forest and when I went back to search for her kind, I found none. Will you help her?" asked Lady MacQuellion.

Tulon nodded. He'd help her, but not the way Lady MacQuellion was thinking.

"You brute. You big, disgusting, boorish man. I hate you," screeched Rowena, throwing her bowl of water in his face.

Tulon shook his head. *What did I do now*? Women, they mystified him. This one irritated him like a blister under his hooves.

"I said I'd help, but I will not rut with her," he said, speaking to Lady MacQuellion, while ignoring the fuming woman at his side.

Lady MacQuellion moved to her daughter's side by the hearth. "What do you have in mind?"

"She can travel with us through the forest. I know where her kin live," he said. Tulon hoped that the Betikhan were still there. He had come across their summer village as he wandered through the Dark Forest. They were nomadic and never stayed too long in one place.

He watched Felicia stand, making sure to gather as much of the fur covering as she could close to her skin. Then Tulon knew without a doubt he had to get her to her kin. She was embarrassed at what she was. That was a true shame.

"You will take me with you. You will find my kin," said Felicia.

Tulon noted it was a statement, not a question. The oddity of that struck Tulon's heart. He knew she, like Rowena, cursed her femininity. They were both plagued with the itch for sex. He could have laughed at his own predicament, but his cock still throbbed from the young Betikhan's skillful tongue.

"How old are you?" he asked, needing to learn more about the creature he had willingly agreed to help.

"I judge her to be about eighteen cycles," answered Lady MacQuellion, providing a wooden bowl filled with cool water for her daughter.

Tulon all but growled in frustration. Now more than ever he knew he could never sexually fulfill her. She needed a powerful Mage Betikhan, a male in his prime who could seep his magic into her—bonding them for eternity. Without a Mage mate, she would die. No amount of rutting on his part would cure her.

"I will provide two of my best Tree Wraiths to guide you," said Lady MacQuellion, moving to the hut's door.

"Thank you, but that will not be necessary," answered Tulon.

"Actually, I think that's a great idea," replied Rowena, moving away from Tulon.

He grabbed her arm and pulled her closer to him. "No, it is not!" He growled the words seductively low for her ears only, hoping the young Betikhan wouldn't pay any attention to the command in his voice.

"Why not?" she mouthed.

"Because he knows I will mate with them and he knows that's not a good idea," answered Felicia, taking a sip from the bowl.

"How so?"

"It's simple," answered Tulon. "Once she mates with a creature other than a Mage Betikhan, they die."

"You mean to say that if you had agreed to her request, you'd be dead?" Rowena's eyes grew large with fear.

Tulon nodded.

"And you knew that from the get-go, didn't you?" she stated, giving his shoulder a good solid punch. Her anger caused her almost naked skin to turn a delicious shade of cinnamon pink. His instinct was to reach out and lick her. Instead, he grabbed her body tight to his.

"Enough, Rowena," he said, whispering the words into her ear. By her body's shudder, he knew he had her complete attention. "She will accompany us and we will move quickly through the forest to find her kin."

Just how quickly, they had no idea. When the opportunity arose, he planned to give in to his own need and flash into a stallion. The call to do so was singing through his blood.

"That's just great, but what about me? What about..." Here she stumbled, too ashamed to admit her own personal crisis.

Inhaling her fresh, orange-lemony scent instantly thickened his shaft more. With her body pressed up to his, he knew she felt his desire. "I will take care of you."

"You're driving me nuts," she snapped, breaking free from him to move to the stone hearth, closer to Felicia.

Her words hit home with Tulon. *What by the Saints am I thinking?* For the first time in a long time, not of himself. That made him mad.

Maybe I should give in to this hunger and take the opportunity to ram Rowena to bliss. What's wrong with being a little selfish?

Deep down, he knew ramming Rowena only once wasn't going to alleviate his desire and that notion didn't sit well with him either.

Chapter Seven

"Does he ever talk?" asked Felicia.

Rowena noted she wore a light brown fur top that concealed her chest. She hadn't bothered to cover up her fawn legs. The sight of them still caused Rowena to gulp and blink all at once. In truth, she wasn't sure how many more myths or legends coming to life she could stand.

"Let's just say he's not a conversationalist," she answered.

As much as Rowena disliked sharing her own crisis, the knowledge that the young Betikhan walking beside her was facing the same end, in a slightly different way, bonded them together.

"Is he your lover?"

The Betikhan's frank talk caused Rowena to blush. "No," she replied more frantically than she intended.

"He likes you," stated Felicia, stopping to pick a bright orange flower that had small red berries.

Rowena watched as Felicia popped it into her mouth and ate it, stem and all. The flower was the same type of plant she had watched Tulon pop into his mouth. Obviously it was edible. Grasping one of the plants by the stem, she pulled hard and placed it in her mouth.

"Yuck." She attempted to spit out as much of the bitter plant as she could. "That's disgusting. How can you eat that?"

"I'm Betikhan. To me, they taste wonderful," answered Felicia, popping two more for show into her mouth.

"Will you two stop talking and move it," commanded Tulon, ducking under and over branches as nimble as could be.

Not so for Rowena. No longer wearing the sheer see-through dress, she was garbed in simple breeches and a tunic. Hard leather sandals adorned her feet.

Tulon wore black breeches and a black tunic, but he had preferred to go barefoot. The simplicity of his clothes and the color suited him like a glove. He was also the only one armed. Lady MacQuellion had given him her bow and arrows as a going away gift.

Rowena had felt humbled as Lady MacQuellion openly wept when they left. To Lady MacQuellion, she had been saying goodbye to her one and only daughter. So what if she hadn't given birth to the girl. Rowena knew Felicia had found a place in Lady MacQuellion's heart forever.

They had been traveling for half of the morning and gone about four klicks. The underbrush of the forest was getting thicker and harder to wind through. A few times Tulon had turned them around, forcing them to backtrack and go around a large knot of impenetrable trees.

When he held up his hand to silence them, she stilled.

What does he hear? She strained her ears for any noise besides the eerie silence of the Dark Forest.

"We need to move, something is coming our way," he said, plunging his way through the forest.

Rowena shivered. She didn't like the Dark Forest and she especially disliked the things that seemed to materialize out of nowhere.

When a snake-vine attempted to twine its way around her leg, she screamed. Immediately, Tulon was at her side. He slammed his foot down hard on the vine and instantly it went limp.

Grateful, Rowena opened her mouth to say thank you.

"I told you to move it. Now!" he commanded, roughly yanking her forward.

The man doesn't deserve my thanks. "Let go of me," she said, huffing as he continued to drag her through the forest. A quick look around and she realized Felicia was nowhere in sight.

"Where did Felicia go?" she asked, fearing they had somehow gotten separated.

"She's ahead of us. I told her to run. She knows what's coming after us, so she didn't hesitate."

"What's coming after us?" asked Rowena, hating her own curiosity.

"The forest," he stated, never once letting go of his hold on her arm.

Rowena wanted to ask what that meant, but she didn't need to. Behind her, she could see exactly what he was talking about. Large trees were uplifting their roots to lumber after them, while vines slashed forward like a horsewhip toward them.

"Run," she screamed, as a large tree to Tulon's right attempted to grab him with its large branches.

He narrowly dodged it, still dragging her along.

"Once we make it past the river, we will be safe." Tulon picked up speed as he easily sidestepped the trees' advances.

"I don't think we're going to make it," shouted Rowena, willing her legs to move faster. A cramp in her side restricted her breathing. To stop, though, was certain death.

Abruptly she felt Tulon grab her, forcing her to a standstill.

"What are you doing? We can't stop," she said, panting from fear and exertion, as she tried to break free from his grip.

"Look down," he said, killing another vine with his foot.

"By the Saints," said Rowena, her breath catching in her throat. They were standing on the precipice of a cliff and down was a good sixty feet. Death loomed all around them. Instinctively, she moved closer to Tulon.

"Okay, macho-man, just how do you propose we get out of this one alive?" she asked.

"We pray," he said.

Rowena didn't like that answer. She had never been a great believer and the power of prayer was beyond her. Now, however, she silently recited every prayer she could, hoping for a miracle.

Tulon sought the magic within him. Then he threw back his head and bellowed as loudly as he could, wondering if it would do any good. Things certainly didn't look good for them. *And where, by the Saints, is Felicia?* If she had taken the same route as they had, she should be here with them. He hoped she had found a way down the cliff, but highly doubted that.

Two more lumbering trees came at him. He backed up and moved to the right, putting more space between him and Rowena.

The answering cry from the skies was a welcome relief. His friend Rusty was coming to the rescue. *Now if only he'd kick those wings of his into high gear.* Tulon once again shifted to the right to lure the trees away from Rowena. A rush of wind cascaded through his hair.

"Fancy seeing you here. What's it been? Let me think... almost two years and you're still running around as a two-legged."

Rusty's hollow laughter as he swooped in low to almost kick him in the head didn't amuse Tulon.

"I'll explain it all later. Save the woman!" he yelled, choosing to ignore the jab about his human form, as he jumped to narrowly avoid becoming pulpwood by the angry trees that were seeking revenge for their trespassing through the forest.

"You mean that woman," taunted his friend, flying low once again to jeer at Tulon.

Tulon looked to his left. All he could see were Rowena's hands as she gripped with all her might at a fallen log that hung over the cliff.

"Blast it, Rusty, get her. Now!" yelled Tulon, frustration eating him raw.

"As you command," said his friend, elegantly bowing low in mid-flight.

The mockery of that wasn't lost on Tulon.

In truth, Tulon was surprised his friend had come at all. Their friendship went back a long time, but Rusty wasn't known for his dependability or acts of chivalry. He had always been a loner like him. As a warrior of the Mage Pegcentaurs, he was highly flighty by nature.

The fact he was the only one Tulon had confided in about his current stallion or man predicament said a lot about the trust he had for him. After wandering alone in the forest for two months, he'd almost gone mad with talking to himself, so he hadn't hesitated to rant about all that had happened to him.

Thanking the Saints that Rusty had been close, he prayed he had made the right decision. Then again, one glance at the sheer drop below the cliff informed him that he hadn't had any other choice.

When Rowena screamed in surprise, Tulon breathed a sigh of relief. At least she was safe. He, on the other hand, was in the fight of his life. More trees moved toward him, edging him closer to the cliff. What could he do? The hairs on his arms stood on end. All of his keen senses told him the underside of the cliff wasn't secure, but alas, he had nowhere else to run.

His arms spiraled backward as he tried to level himself, but it didn't help.

"Need some help, buddy?" asked Rusty, his large wings buffeting Tulon from falling backward.

"That would be great," answered Tulon, wondering what exactly he would have to do to ever live this moment down.

"It will cost you," taunted Rusty.

"By the Saints, save him!" screeched Rowena.

"Stop kicking me, woman, or you will be sorry!" shouted Rusty. "This is one cantankerous woman you've asked me to save, Tulon. Are you sure you don't want me to drop her? Then the two of us could go to Mount Atrophe for lots of pleasuring. Lady, if you so much as twitch that foot of yours, you will no longer be on my back. Am I clear?"

"Clear. Now save him," demanded Rowena.

Tulon smiled. Even when she was faced with the unknown and her very life was at stake, the feisty spitfire held firm to her convictions.

"Should I save you, Tulon?" asked Rusty.

"That would be nicer than letting my bits and pieces be eaten by the birds," replied Tulon, trying once again to get his footing on the cliff.

"In return for saving you, you will take me to Iris."

"You know I cannot—"

Before he could finish that sentence, the ground shook beneath him and he fell from the cliff. Wind whipped around him as he gave in to the freefall and then two strong hands grasped him—Rusty's.

Vaulting over his friend's head, he mounted, holding tight to Rowena whose entire body shook with fear.

Tulon's nose caught the scent of green grass before he spotted the lush meadow. A herd of Mage Pegcentaurs greeted them. *That isn't good.* In their midst stood one awestruck Felicia. Her eyes were wide and her mouth gaped as she admired the four-legged magical creatures that commanded both the air and the meadows of the First Haven.

Thankful that the Dark Forest was behind them, Tulon let the magic of his homeland invade his senses. A sigh of contentment escaped him.

As Tulon dismounted from Rusty, Rowena threw herself into his arms. "What is it?" she squeaked in his ear.

"Did that woman ask 'what is it'?" asked his friend.

Tulon quickly set aside Rowena. The last thing he wanted was for Rusty to get mad. He had always had a short fuse and once riled, he was hard to settle.

"Rowena, this is Rusty, my most trusted friend. He's a Mage Pegcentaur," said Tulon, as he forced Rowena to give a stiff bow. Thankful for once that she didn't fight him, he breathed a sigh of relief.

"She is a humanoid," snorted Rusty, "with pointy heels."

"Sorry about kicking you. I was scared and confused. I'm not sure I follow what exactly you are," said Rowena

Before his friend and those around him could snort their disdain for her bad manners, Tulon interjected. "Rowena is a Maida woman from the land beyond the Dark Forest. Felicia, are you okay?" asked Tulon, as the young Betikhan moved toward them, thankful for the interruption.

She nodded, clearly too stunned to speak.

"Felicia is Betikhan and we were trying to get her to her kin, when the forest decided that they'd had enough of us," sneered Tulon.

"Betikhan, did you say? We saw them two hundred wing beats away," answered a young Pegcentaur to Tulon's right.

"I saved her. She was trying to swim through the current. She must be daft," said the young Pegcentaur with disdain.

"I am not daft, you hybrid!" snapped Felicia, who chose that moment to finally snap out of her shell-shocked state.

"Who are you calling a hybrid?" snarled the young Pegcentaur.

"Enough. Hilt, thank you for saving her," said Rusty, eyeing the young Pegcentaur. "Tulon, Hilt is correct. We can take her to her kin if you'd like," answered Rusty, "after you take me to Iris."

"Iris does not want to see you," snapped Tulon, shaking his head.

"Ooh, yes, she does. It's your blasted stepfather that doesn't want to see me," answered his friend. "And does this woman know what you really are?"

If anything had been in his hand, he would have attempted to smack his friend. Discretion had never been one of his strong suits, but the last thing he wanted was to get into a discussion about himself.

"What are you talking about? He's a man," stated Rowena, eyeing his friend like he had two heads.

Before he could say anything else, his friend flashed into human form. Gone were his two large white wings, his horse body and half-man chest, head and arms. Tulon swore in all the languages he knew, which was quite a lot. *Show-off*! He eyed the tall, imposing red-haired giant who now stood before them.

"Oh my," said Rowena, breathily, as she scanned Rusty's body with keen interest.

"Is she really a Maida woman? Is her pussy as good as they say?" asked his friend, eyeing Rowena lewdly.

Instantly, Tulon rose to the challenge. Yanking Rowena to him, he turned his eyes on his friend, his tone anything but warm. "She is not for you."

"But he might be able to—"

Tulon clamped his mouth over Rowena's lips to silence her. The last thing he wanted her to admit to was her sexual itch that was screaming for relief. He brought her body flush to his. Angling her head with his hand, he set out to mark her as his.

When her two arms snaked around his head to tighten her grip on him, he plunged his tongue into her inviting mouth. She sighed in pleasure. Her leg wrapped around his, almost toppling them to the grass, as desire shot like an arrow straight to his hard, throbbing shaft.

A loud applause greeted him, causing him to release his hold on her mouth. When he looked up, all of the Pegcentaurs had flashed into male humans. Well-endowed male humans. Tulon snorted in anger, as he heard Rowena's very aroused sigh of "Oh my".

Setting aside a clearly stunned Rowena, Tulon moved to his friend's side.

"She doesn't know," said Rusty, as he gripped his friend's forearms in a warrior-to-warrior embrace.

Tulon didn't want to admit it, but the idea of telling Rowena what he was terrified him. He knew he would see that mortified look on her face. As much as she had befriended Felicia, a part of her had kept her distance from the young Betikhan.

"Tell her. And yes, you will take me to Iris," commanded his friend, walking away, his ass gleaming in the sun.

Tulon didn't need to look at Rowena. He knew she was watching all of the men intently. That infuriated the blazes out of him. He didn't want her looking at other men. Her eyes should only be for him. However, with a herd of primed naked men, some whose shafts were already jumping to attention with just the scent of the Maida woman, he couldn't condemn her actions. But he certainly didn't have to like them. Or her, for that matter.

Running to keep up with his friend, he made him halt, knowing he had left Rowena and Felicia alone. Things needed to be said. And he didn't want Rowena to overhear him.

"Rusty, I've been gone for over two years and, as much as I'd like to go home, I can't."

"Why not?" asked his friend, still trudging forward.

Tulon bowed his head in frustration. It rankled him that he would have to admit to being banished. "I was banished from the clan."

"For what?"

"What do you mean, for what?" asked Tulon.

Rusty finally stopped to turn and look at him. "What did you do to your clan that made them banish you?"

All of Tulon's hairs stood on end. He was angry. "I didn't do a blasted thing to my clan. I was banished because I'm not a Centaur." Silently, he thought about admitting that his stepfather had banished him because he looked too much like his father, but Rusty would simply snort "I told you so". He had always hated Rython because the proud Centaur wouldn't let him date Tulon's younger sister, Iris.

"What are you talking about? You're still a Centaur. You just haven't figured out how to utilize the magic yet," stated his friend in his no-nonsense tone.

"Easy for you to say. You can flash without a problem. When I flash, it's either into a stallion or a man, never both."

"It wasn't always easy for me, Tulon. When we first met, I couldn't fly," admitted his friend.

"What?"

"That's right. I couldn't fly."

Tulon ached to remove his breeches to have the feel of the crisp, green grass touch his body. "But you're a Mage Pegcentaur. You fly and wield magic as you wish."

"Yes and no. Now I am a Mage Pegcentaur, but it took a while for me to learn to harness the magic so that I could fly. And it wasn't easy. I made many mistakes. Some very painful, but I never gave up," stated his friend, turning his back to Tulon to move forward again.

"Are you implying I gave up?" asked Tulon, briskly moving after his friend.

"You said it. I didn't," taunted Rusty, jumping out of Tulon's reach.

Chapter Eight

"I think I must be dreaming," said Rowena, turning to find Felicia flanking her right.

"Then that makes two of us," said Felicia. "You know, those men are really good-looking."

Rowena turned to stare at the young Betikhan. "Don't even think of having sex with one of them," she said, mortified she had to mention that to Felicia.

"I didn't say I'd have sex with them. I just want to play," taunted Felicia, moving away from Rowena before she could grab her.

Play. That's just great. She wants to play while I ache for sex. Then it dawned on Rowena that maybe this was all an elaborate hallucination brought on by her lack of sexual fulfillment. The degeneration of her brain cells had already started. *That's it. I really am losing my mind.*

The sight of the naked men, all of whom were well-muscled in just the right places and very well endowed did nothing to quench her need. She wet her lips instinctively, while plopping down on the ground. What she really wanted to do was jump one of their bones—preferably one with a long, hard shaft. *That bone will do the job perfectly.* She grimaced at her own racy thoughts.

When Tulon plopped down beside her, she fought the urge to beat at him in frustration. It wasn't his fault she felt like she did—emotionally a wreck. Tears fell unheeded down her cheeks.

On top of that, she could clearly see what Felicia meant about playing. In the wide-open meadow, everything was on display. There was no privacy, not that the Pegcentaurs seemed to mind.

And did I just really say that—Pegcentaurs! Really, I must be losing it. They don't exist. It's just another myth. Rowena thought hard, trying to formulate a scientific reason for what she was witnessing. They certainly looked real enough to her, but she was starting to doubt her own sanity.

"Don't worry, they know what she is and they won't overstep their bounds," said Tulon, wiping away her tears.

His light touch sent a shiver of anticipation straight to her clenching core muscles.

"That little thing has a very skillful tongue."

Immediately Rowena's anger surged to the surface. "That's disgusting. You're disgusting. I hate you," she said, standing so she could run away from him.

When he stood and grasped both of her arms and tossed her to the warm ground she fought him like a hellcat. She bucked, scratched and hollered at him. When he didn't relent, but kept her pinned between his hard thighs, she finally stilled. Turning her head to her left, she watched as Felicia took a long, hard shaft of one of the Pegcentaurs deep within her mouth.

"Why don't you join the line for some of that?" she spat.

"What I want is that pussy of yours," taunted Tulon.

Rowena tried to buck him off her again. *This is futile.* They had already been down that long, hot, steamy path and it only left her aching for more. Oh sure, the brief climax had refueled her sex-crazed cells, but it hadn't taken long for that itch to resurface with a vengeance. She most certainly didn't want to meet bliss again only to have to deal with hell later.

When Tulon leaned over her, so that his wild, forest scent cascaded through her, she moaned from the heady, musky smell of him.

Two dark chocolate eyes seared her with their heat. His look caused her to blush.

"What I really want, spitfire, is to first suckle those breasts of yours until you are so wet I can slide my cock deep inside you so you know what it feels like to be taken, ridden and pleasured. But before I do that, I plan to lick that warm pussy cream of yours with my tongue. I plan to make you scream with wanting me," he said, his breath warm on her ear.

His words did more to excite her than she thought possible. For once, all reason fled. Turning her eyes up at him, she notched up her chin. "I dare you," she taunted, thinking, to death with the consequences.

Daring him was the last thing Tulon had expected from Rowena. He almost wished he hadn't pushed her so far but he wasn't about to back down from the challenge. This one excited him beyond reason.

The fact she did it knowing they were on display tantalized the beast within. Of course, the honorable part of him had no intention of taking her where every creature could spy on them. Truthfully, he didn't like the idea of anyone else but him seeing her naked body. Sharing had never come easily to him and he had no intention of letting anyone glimpse a morsel of her silky skin.

"Do you know what you are asking?" He watched as her chest rose and fell. Clad in the tight-fitting tunic, the outline of her breasts teased him. He knew what they felt and tasted like and he didn't like the barrier that separated him from her succulent buds.

Rowena didn't say anything.

Great, the one time I'm hoping to be talked out of something and she's silent, go figure. Mesmerized, he watched as she slowly nodded her head and licked her red lips. It was too much for him.

He groaned as he lowered his head—knowing he would claim her, here and now. Bringing the magic of his being to life, he shielded them as he kissed her, plunging his tongue over and over again into her inviting mouth. Her answering tongue dueled with his, spurring on the untamed part of him.

He felt her petite hands slide into his hair and goose bumps formed all over his sensitive skin as her fingers caressed his mane of hair. The sensation was unlike any other he had experienced. Never once breaking the kiss, he made short work of the hooks clasping her tunic together and in no time her bare breasts were molded to his hands.

Tulon loved how she moaned and writhed underneath him as he stroked both of her nipples with his fingers. Even though he shielded them from prying eyes, the sun and the light breeze filtered through his shield. Immediately, her nipples puckered to attention from the late-day breeze.

Moving from her lips, his hands lifted her breasts so he could feast on them. He took one deep within his mouth and suckled hard, knowing she felt the pull deep within her womb. Once he was satisfied that one breast had received enough attention, he moved to the second, loving how she arched her back, inviting his tongue to lavish unyielding attention to her sensitive peaks.

Even though she thought they were on display, she wasn't inhibited with her cries of pleasure. That shocked him, while causing his cock to grow even more rigid. His stones were so tight with need, they hurt. Being tightly confined in breeches didn't help matters. And before he knew what he had done, they were both naked. His magic was pulsing all around him and he was slowly losing control. Thankfully, Rowena was oblivious to what had happened.

When her small hand grasped his hard cock, he threw back his head in ecstasy. The feel of her warm skin on his was an aphrodisiac. The air around them all but crackled as his magic raced to the surface. Gritting his teeth, Tulon knew he had no choice. He had to have her. He wouldn't be denied.

When Rowena spread her legs wider, her musky, wet scent caused his nostrils to flare. Holding her arms above her head, he moved lower, kissing and nipping her bare flesh—loving that she was on display for him. With his head nestled between her soft, brown curls, he stroked her clit. Her pussy was already wet and ready for him. Her cream was delectable and called to him. Opening her folds with his finger, he lapped at her nectar, wanting to prolong the moment for as long as he could, while enjoying the play of the game.

"More, Tulon, more. I can't stand another second of it." She moaned, trying to lift her upper half off the grass.

Pinning her arms to her side, he stilled her movements while darting his tongue deep inside her wet opening. She tasted like sweet, warm, fresh honey. He loved how her cream coated his own lips. It made him hunger for more.

"Tulon, please," she begged and whimpered, tossing her head back as pleasure rode her.

This was the part he loved. Bringing a female to climax, watching as pleasure surfaced throughout her whole body. It was a gift. It would be his gift to her and this time he planned to welcome it. He stroked her wet opening with his fingers. Pebbling her nub until it hardened and ached, he watched with male satisfaction as her body reached the precipice and then got swept away.

"By the Saints, oh my, oh my, ohmymy..." panted Rowena, as she came.

Her wet cream slid down his throat as his tongue licked her dry. Her taste was now fully implanted in his being and he knew he would kill any that tried to sample what was his.

"Tulon," she moaned.

He didn't want to think about his actions, so he didn't hesitate. Positioning himself between her legs, he looked up, noting the fear in her sky-blue eyes. He knew she was having doubts but he didn't want to explain that everything would be okay. He simply wanted to claim all of her.

"Tulon," she breathed, and before she could say anything more, he nudged her folds open with the tip of his cock and plunged deep inside her tight opening. He stilled, letting her body get used to the feel of him deep within her. Then he slowly withdrew only to slide deliciously, inch by thick inch, back into her hot pussy.

He felt her hands on his back as she pulled at him, wanting all of him deep inside her and that spurred him on. Without further finesse, he plunged in deeper, and then he rode her hard. Deep, long, thorough strokes that brought instant heat to her body.

"Come for me again, Rowena. Fly with me," he said, loving how she instinctively wrapped her long, silky legs around him, urging him on.

"Harder," she panted, her nails raking his back, while she grasped his ass with her legs.

He loved that she liked it wild. She reminded him of the fillies on Mount Atrophe.

Tucking his hands under her ass, he lifted her hips, allowing him even deeper penetration. He swore he could touch her womb and her wet, hot heat was slowly eroding all of his control. Before he climaxed, he wanted her to join him, so he circled his hips, knowing the sensation would nudge her secret sensitive spot, while his cock screamed for release.

"Oh mymymy!" cried Rowena, arching up off the grass, to grip his back harder as she climaxed again and flew to her own pleasure.

Tulon threw back his head, roaring his satisfaction, as he pumped his seed deep inside her womb. He loved how her pussy muscles milked him for all he was worth.

Careful not to position all of his weight on her, he leaned down to tenderly kiss her. She held him tight to her chest. Tears ran freely down her cheeks. He hoped they were tears of joy.

"I'm so sorry, Tulon," mumbled Rowena into his shoulder.

Then she turned her head to finally look at him. Her blue eyes were rimmed with pools of salty tears.

"I'm not sorry, Rowena, so why are you?" he said, hating he had kept secret that he wasn't Maida.

"You're going to die," she said, sniffling on even more tears.

"No, I'm not," he said, sheepishly. He ached to tell her the truth.

Before he could say another thing, a loud piercing whistle sliced through the air.

"What was that?" asked Rowena, trying to poke her head over his shoulder. "By the Saints, where are we?"

Finally withdrawing from her, Tulon looked around at his surroundings. "Blast it," he mumbled. Somehow in the throes of his passion, he had flashed them to Mount Atrophe and that wasn't good.

"Get the two-leggeds," commanded a loud, booming voice that caused all the hairs on his head to stand on end.

Tulon knew he had to get them off Mount Atrophe and fast. Worse, the only safe and quick way was to flash into a stallion.

Turning to look at Rowena, he stilled his heart. "What you're about to see is probably going to scare you, but it's the only thing I can think of that will get us out of here. For once, do as I say," he commanded.

Not waiting for her response, he walked a safe distance away from her. Then, without thinking any more about his actions, he let the magic fuel his cells and willed his body to flash into his true form—a Centaur.

He held his breath, hoping that for once the magic had listened to him. A toss of his mane told him it wasn't so. He was a blasted stallion. He still couldn't control the strange pulse of magic that hummed through his system. Hating what had become of him, he pranced on all fours, all but stomping the lush meadow as anger surged through the marrow of his bones.

"I thought sex was supposed to stop the hallucinations," giggled Rowena, still sitting on the grass.

Tossing his mane, he pawed the ground again. Lifting his head, he let the magic run wild within him, not caring that he couldn't control some of it, as a red haze of power floated above him. He had never felt more frustrated in his life.

His keen senses told him that the Gaffelion warriors were fast approaching. He pawed the ground again, willing her to understand that she had to mount him so they could leave. If they didn't, and if she was caught, she'd be killed without a second glance.

Prancing closer, he knelt down, wondering what she would do.

The last thing he expected was a sweet sigh, as she leaned her head into his velvety smooth mane and stroked him.

"You're not really Maida, are you?" she asked.

He snorted. Nodding his head, Tulon hated that he couldn't communicate with her. His sensitive ears could discern that the Gaffelion warriors were almost upon them. Nudging her to get on his back, he thanked the Saints when she complied.

Once she had a firm grip of his thick mane, he galloped off, loving the feel and smell of her still naked flesh on his. When she wrapped her hands around his neck, the feel of her breasts bouncing on him caused him to think of all the delicious things he would like to do with her now that she wasn't repulsed by him being a stallion.

However what he really wanted to be able to show her was what he had been—a Centaur. Frustrated by his lack of ability to control the magic, he forced his legs to pick up the pace, knowing they had a long, hard ride ahead of them if they were going to join the Pegcentaur clan by nightfall. By then, Rowena would be tired and sore. Once he flashed back into a human, he planned to kiss away every ache on her delectable flesh.

Chapter Nine

Rowena figured she had been having the best erotic dream of her life. Mind-shattering, melt your bones, yummy sex that had her sensitive clit aching for more and her hot core muscles clenching in anticipation, and now this.

She was riding a black, velvety smooth stallion, bare ass and all. And it wasn't just any stallion. It was Tulon.

Without a doubt, she knew all of her brain cells had completely degenerated. In truth, she was simply waiting for all her other bodily functions to start to shut down. But before that happened, she figured why not enjoy it while it lasted.

With her thighs spread over Tulon's wide back, she bumped along as his pace picked up. Her breasts, aching with renewed need, bounced up and down and sometimes sideways as she held on for dear life. She had no idea what was after them, but if Tulon was running from it, she knew it was bad.

When he reared up on his hind legs, she scrambled for a tighter hold of his thick, midnight mane.

Then she saw them. A hysterical, high-pitched crazed laugh took hold of her.

In front of her had to be the most mixed-up creatures she had ever seen. Four of the large creatures stood directly in front of her and Tulon. Each had a giraffe's body with long legs and a long neck, but they had a lion's tail, two small wings that looked incapable of flight, and their faces were in the shape of a lion's, equipped with a thick golden mane.

What shocked her more was that one of them spoke and she could understand it. She had expected it would either neigh or roar at her, but hearing clipped, civilized words stream eloquently from its muzzle freaked her out.

"We know it's you, Tulon. Your scent gives you away," said the largest of the creatures as it restlessly pawed the ground.

Tulon lowered himself to the ground. Taking that as her cue to dismount, Rowena did just that. Hiding herself behind Tulon, she blushed at her nakedness from her toes to the roots of her short-cropped hair.

A blinding white flash was her only warning and then Tulon materialized next to her in human form, looking not one bit pleased with the situation.

"What are they?" she whispered.

"Those are Gaffelions. They are guardians of Mount Atrophe. They are beastly," said Tulon. "Magel, go away," he snapped, dismissing the strange creature.

When Tulon took in her state of undress, she shook from his heated intense look. When he touched her shoulder, heat slammed into her body as a part of whatever he was seeped into her being. Before she knew it, she was once again fully clothed in her breeches, tunic and sandals.

"Thank you," she said, feeling more in control of herself.

"You know I have to take you to Fredia, our Beloved Pleasure Mistress," said the creature who Tulon had called Magel.

"Can't you just wish us out of here?" asked Rowena, wondering what type of powers Tulon had.

Tulon simply shook his head.

Turning her attention to the weird creatures, Rowena asked the obvious. "Okay, why won't you let us leave? We didn't mean to come here and we really need to be on our way," she stated in her no-nonsense tone of voice. She notched her chin up as she started to move forward.

Tulon hauled her closer to him.

"You're a two-legged. No two-leggeds are allowed on Mount Atrophe. The punishment is most severe," said Magel, with a crooked smile that looked ridiculous on a lion's face.

"I am sick of all of this, Tulon. None of this makes any sense to me," said Rowena, flapping her arms in the air, exasperated beyond means. "All I wanted to do was help you escape and so far I've met more myths and legends that have come true than I can stomach. And, this," she turned her attention back to the crazy creatures, "this makes no sense whatsoever."

Trying to muster her courage, she disgraced herself when a loud sniffle gave her away. Tears began to stream down her cheeks. Frustrated and at her limit, Rowena wanted more than anything to indulge in her own self-pity act. Brushing off Tulon's gentle hand on her shoulder, she stalked away only to come face-to-face with a magnificent creature.

"Kneel, woman!" shouted Magel.

Rowena turned her head to look at Tulon. He stood regally tall, not bothering to bend even a finger at the imposing creature standing before them. Only when two Gaffelions forced him to kneel on the ground, did she follow suit, scrambling to her knees and bowing her head in submission.

A bright red flash fell over the entire meadow and when Rowena next peeked, gone was the magnificent unicorn and in its place was a man. His skin was the color of midnight and he gleamed as if he had been coated with gold fairy dust. He was all muscle in all the right places and his piercing green eyes fixed themselves on her.

Instantly she felt heat pool to her core. The need to rub herself almost caused her to move her own hand to her wet pussy. She flinched, fighting his sexual attraction.

Next to her, Tulon looked up and groaned.

"Tulon, you have brought me a gift. Thank you. You may rise."

The man had a rich deep voice and accent, which caused Rowena's nipples to peak to attention. It was the same reaction she had when Tulon spoke. *Not that I would ever admit that to him.*

"She is not for you, Prince," said Tulon, moving closer to Rowena.

"So you say. Let us see."

"Prince?" Rowena squeaked as she eyed the man who was now advancing toward her. She tried hard to will her eyes to look elsewhere, but his shaft was impressive. Sex all but oozed off him.

"I see you still haven't mastered your powers, Tulon. That's a shame," sneered the man.

"Oh, shut up," snapped Tulon.

Immediately, two of the strange Gaffelions surrounded him. "Show respect to your prince," commanded Magel.

"He's not my prince. He's yours. Cut the games. You don't need us, so let us go," said Tulon, ignoring the growling beings flanking his sides.

When the prince stood opposite her, Rowena caught his scent and all but swooned. Wild woods, wet streams and a visual image of him taking her in the water caused her to moan.

"Rowena," said Tulon, shaking his head.

"You know, Tulon, I think she likes me a lot," said the man, and before she knew it, her clothing had once again disappeared. Bare to the wind, she fought the urge to run.

"You lay a finger on her and you are dead," growled Tulon, positioning himself between her and the strange man in a blink that caused both of the Gaffelion creatures that had been flanking him to start in surprise.

The very air around Rowena crackled with energy. A hum of something ominous sounded around them as a red glow emanated from Tulon. Afraid of what was happening to him, she backed away.

"You think you can take me on, Tulon, go ahead," taunted the man, holding out his hands. Pitch-black energy surrounded him.

When Rowena next looked, both Tulon and the man were gone. She was alone with the crazy Gaffelion creatures. And she didn't like the way they were eyeing her naked flesh like she was dessert.

* * * * *

Tulon had never before experienced such uncontrolled rage. He felt a powerful surge of magic flow into his body and a keen knowledge of how to wield it tickled at his subconscious. The power almost terrified him. But not quite.

He had been bested once by the so-called Prince of the Forest, his old nemesis, Zickal, but now it was an entirely different matter. He would not let Zickal touch one inch of Rowena's bare skin. Without a doubt, he would kill him if he had to.

"You were always so predictable, Tulon," sneered Zickal.

Tulon grinned. He liked familiar ground, and that's exactly what the Plains had become to him over the years. The wide-open space beckoned to him to run wild. The Plains had been his home for years while he trained to become a Centaur warrior. It was here that he had first met Zickal, a mere Centaur, before he had been crowned prince by the Mage Saints of the Forest after Zickal had undergone his *thrush* two years ago.

That had been the same morning when Tulon had awoken only to discover he was a stallion or a man and could never hold the magic long enough to become Centaur again. Something else leapt through his mind, but he chose to ignore it.

"So, you want to fight the traditional way," taunted Tulon, loving how the flow of power felt warm and inviting on his skin.

"You know, I had something a bit more dangerous in mind. But you're probably not Centaur enough to handle it."

Tulon took two steps toward Zickal so they stood face-to-face. The air around them crackled as the force of their magic touched.

"Name it," snapped Tulon, simply wanting to get on with it.

"Okay, my challenge is that whoever can get the Maida woman to climax three times gets to have her for good," said Zickal, eyeing Tulon.

Tulon knew Rowena wasn't his to bargain with. Worse, if she knew what he was about to agree to, she'd hate him forever. But he liked the idea of giving in to the darker side of his nature and, without a doubt, he was determined to win this wager.

He nodded. "Okay, but I don't plan on being here for eternity, so let's sweeten the bargain. Whoever can get the woman to climax three times by the cresting of the dawning sun claims her and gets safe passage out of here. Is that clear?"

"As you wish," taunted Zickal.

Tulon would have liked nothing better than to knock the so-called Prince of the Forest on his ass. Instead, he reached up to clasp Zickal in the traditional warrior greeting to seal their bargain.

Stepping away from Zickal, Tulon didn't like the gleam in his eye. Before he could ponder anything further, his nemesis flashed away to who knew where. Tulon growled in frustration. *So be it. Let the chase begin.*

Chapter Ten

Rowena rubbed her eyes. One minute she was eyeing the four Gaffelions who seemed to be stalking her, and then in the next moment she found herself standing knee-deep in a pool of warm light blue water. To her right was a small waterfall and to her left was a grassy bank that was home to wild pink and white roses. She fought against the urge to sneeze. She hated roses. The scent of them reminded her of her aunts and that wasn't pleasant.

"So, my lovely, you are called Rowena and you are Maida. It is a pleasure to meet you," said the prince.

Rowena hadn't even seen him. She had been so intent on trying to figure out where she was that she hadn't even noticed him, lazily leaning against a large boulder—naked, casually stroking his thick, long shaft.

How by the Saints did I miss him? His skin gleamed like the color of midnight, his long blond hair streamed to his shoulders and his green eyes stared hungrily at her. Rowena tried to look everywhere but at him. She turned her back to him and then she felt the crackle of energy singe her skin. He was a breath away from her now.

"You are a lovely sight to behold. Your breasts would fit perfectly in my hands. Ahh, I see they, too, like me," said the prince.

Rowena turned away from him. She knew what he was trying to do. Like Tulon, his deep baritone voice had taken on a seductive quality that went straight to her pussy. And his words had caused her nipples to harden to pebbled buds. She shook her head. She wasn't interested in him, she kept telling herself.

"So, where's Tulon?" she asked, keeping her back to him. As least that way he could only eye her ass.

In her crazed desire for sex, simply seeing his chiseled body had quickened her blood, peaked her nipples and caused her core to drip with cream. Mad at her irrational reaction to the prince, man or whatever he was, she fought against the urge to run. There was something about him she didn't like.

"Tulon? Don't you worry your pretty little ass about him. He's fine. I have a gift for you," he said, conjuring a long-stemmed rose in his hand.

Before she had a chance to wonder what it was, she felt his hands skim suggestively over her lower backside, across her bottom and around her midsection as they slowly inched toward her breasts.

"This is for you. I love how your skin pinks with desire. You will be a delight to pleasure," he said, bringing the plucked pink rose closer, so that its petals lightly dusted the crease between her breasts before it was brought to her lips.

"Ahh, ahh choo!" sneezed Rowena.

The look of shock on the prince's face told her that wasn't the reaction he had been expecting. *As if*, she bristled.

"Come here, Rowena."

Now that was a voice she recognized. And as weird as it sounded, simply hearing it brought a flush of warmth to her body and joy to her heart.

Stepping out of the water, she walked to the bank where Tulon stood. Thankfully, he was clothed. She watched as he wet his lips and gulped. The smoldering look in his dark sensual eyes caused a flutter of feminine excitement in her belly.

"I don't think so," said the prince.

Before he had a chance to catch up to her, Tulon was at her side.

"So long, Prince," taunted Tulon, pulling Rowena's body close to his to flash them elsewhere.

They were once again surrounded by the beauty of the forest. Tall green trees towered around them. The scent of wildness, evergreens and damp moss filled her nostrils.

"Come here, Rowena," commanded Tulon, motioning for her to lie down next to him on a green, grassy spot, as if being flashed from place to place was an everyday occurrence for her.

"What's going on, Tulon? Shouldn't we be trying to make a break for it while we can? Can't you just flash us out of here and back to the Pegcentaurs?"

Again he patted the spot beside him. Sitting, she hugged her knees to cover her aching breasts, and only then did he speak, after giving her body another long, heated look. It was all she could do not to splay her legs open for him and tell him to ride her hard.

"I can't flash us out of here, but we are safe for now. I am sorry that you got caught up in this," he said, reaching out to gently trail his fingers up and down her arms.

"You're cold."

Within a moment she felt his heat glide through her. *How does he do that?*

Rowena was getting the sinking feeling that she wasn't delusional after all...that this was actually real. Inwardly, she rebelled at that notion. As a scientist, she knew none of what was happening to her made sense.

Biting on her lower lip, she asked the obvious. "Ooh...so Tulon, what exactly are you?" Rowena had to ask. She felt as if she had been taken on a wild, magical adventure ride, where one amazing, bizarre thing after another kept happening to her.

"I am a Centaur. Well, I used to be," he said, sheepishly. "I will try to make this brief, but all that you need to know is that you are safe with me."

I highly doubt that. Her senses were being lulled into a hazy, sexual feeling of contentment from his seductive voice. When Tulon finished telling her his tale, she gulped.

"You mean to tell me that you were captured by the Maida guards, when in fact you are a magical creature of the forest? Why didn't you flash yourself out of the labor camp?"

Tulon leaned in closer to her. His fingers gently moved from her arm to her face. She let him tilt her face toward his. Their mouths were a breath away from touching. She instinctively wet her lips, wanting very much to feel his powerful mouth take hold of hers.

"Before you came into my life, I honestly felt as if I had stopped living. You made me come alive. You set the magic that simmered within me free. Without you, Rowena, I'm not sure what would have happened to me. Does it scare you that I am different?"

She read the hope in his eyes. "Honestly, I was a little frightened at first, but you haven't changed. You are still Tulon. You are still..."

"Still what?" he said, patting her lower lip with his finger, forcing her to open her mouth in sweet anticipation.

"You are still the only one I want." She felt a sense of freedom with baring her innermost secret.

"Are you sure, Rowena? I need to know that you are sure," he repeated, all the while playing with her lower lip.

Rowena's eyes felt heavy. Her core was weeping for him. So she did the only thing she could. Tilting her head up, she leaned in and kissed him. She slipped her tongue deep inside his mouth and breathed the words she knew he wanted to hear.

"Yes. Take me, Tulon."

That was all the encouragement Tulon needed. The pulse of power thrummed through his being. He reveled in the feel of it. Without a doubt, he knew the magic was slowly talking to him, wielding its secrets into every cell within his being.

He had flashed Rowena and himself to the edge of Mount Atrophe. He had also shielded their presence to ensure Zickal would not be able to track them. Now he planned to fulfill his end of the bargain.

Pushing Rowena down into the soft green grass of the forest he loomed over her—loving the velvety-smooth feel of her womanly body. She was so innocent, so open to his touch that it almost caused him to stop. Then she smiled one of those sexy-shy smiles at him and all reasoning fled.

"Open your legs for me. I want to see your pussy," he rasped, taking her already peaked nipple deep into his mouth. When she did as ordered, he scented her heated arousal, her need, her lust for him. That spurred him on.

"What are you—?"

Tulon silenced her with a kiss that left no doubt as to what he intended. Then he nudged his body between her splayed legs, forcing them to open more. He felt her slight resistance.

"Trust me." Tenderly, he kissed his way down her satiny body. He loved how she squirmed with desire, even as a flush of embarrassment over her exposed body highlighted her flesh. Moving lower, he blew on her hot wet opening. She almost bolted up from the grass, so he used his magic to lock her arms in place over her head.

"Tulon, what are you doing?"

"Pleasuring you well, my spitfire." He grinned, sitting back on his heels to look at her.

She was still arching her neck off the grass to warily watch him. What he wanted to see in those sky-blue eyes of hers was blazing passion.

"Using your magic to hold me down isn't fair play. Ohh," she said, breathlessly.

"So, you are a believer in magic now." Before she could respond to his statement, he grasped her ass and brazenly opened her swollen nether lips with his fingers. She glistened with creamy sex. Still, he wanted more. She panted with need.

The secrets the magic was revealing to him astonished him. Things were starting to make more sense to him from the night he had undergone his *thrush*. However, he forced himself to focus on the task at hand. Grinning, he rocked back on his heels.

"I think your legs are going to be the death of me," he admitted. Before she had time to reply, he once again used his power to position her just the way he wanted.

Her ass was slightly lifted off the ground, her legs were opened wider and her knees were bent to provide him with the perfect angle for his affection. Her pussy glistened at him. Her oomph of surprise became a heady moan when he kissed each cheek.

Her nub gleamed at him...beckoning to him. He planned to taste, suck and devour her hot pussy until she climaxed again and again.

A slow, gentle flick of his tongue on her nub was her first warning. Thankfully, she kept silent. Then he bent his head to her swollen labia lips and laved her as if he were a creature dying of thirst. She tasted like the dewy grass and he loved it. Her moans of desire caused his cock to thicken more and his stones to ache.

"Play with your breasts," he commanded, releasing his magical hold on her arms and lifting his head from her hot core, to ensure she did as instructed.

He read a moment of hesitation in her eyes and then watched as she complied. Her hands roamed over her breasts, brushing the undersides as she pushed them up for his eyes.

"Pinch them," he rasped, as he inserted a finger into her slick opening. What he really wanted to do was ram her with his throbbing cock. Picking up the tempo with his finger, he watched her pinch her nipples to hardened peaks.

"Ohh," she said, slowly becoming more aware of what her body liked.

On her own she raised her ass up to him, inviting his touch. As innocent as she was, there was a wild passion simmering within her waiting for release. Thankfully, he was the right creature for the job.

"Say it," he demanded, blowing on her wet pussy. Her cream was seeping out of her opening like honey and he would like nothing better than to dip his aching cock deep within her nectar.

"Say what?" she croaked, when he once again blew on her swollen lips, the entire time stroking her hard with his finger.

"What do you want me to do, Rowena?" He keenly knew what she wanted, what she needed, but he wanted her to say it.

He waited another minute and then he blew on her nub once more. He chuckled when she tried to buck her ass up even closer to his mouth. She was squirming with the need for release but until she told him exactly what she wanted, he planned to keep up the torture, even though his stones felt as heavy as lead and his cock was jumping to attention.

"Suck me," she said, her face turning crimson with her admission.

It wasn't enough. He wanted her to show him. "Show me what you want me to suck. Show me what your pussy needs," he demanded.

Without preamble, his feisty spitfire sat up, opened her legs wider, reached between her legs and opened her swollen nether lips with her hands. "Suck that," she demanded, tilting her chin up in defiance, knowing she had met his challenge, as she displayed her pink, pebbled nub to him.

"With pleasure."

Cupping her ass with his hands, he took her nub into his mouth and sucked hard, knowing instinctively that she liked it rough.

Freeing one of his hands, he once again stroked her opening. This time he plunged two fingers deep inside her so he could stroke and suck.

"Ohh, yes, oh yes, ohh, mymymy..."

When Rowena came, her juices poured into his mouth. It was the best warm honey cream he had ever tasted. Her body shuddered. Her hands gripped his hair, clasping his head to her core. Only once the shudders subsided and after he had licked her dry did he release her.

"Turn over," he said.

Drowsy, sex filled eyes looked up at him. He knew she was wondering what he wanted, but he held back.

"Trust me," he repeated again, watching as she turned over, her round ass solid and tilted up, as she positioned her arms underneath her.

"On your knees, Rowena," he whispered into her ear.

"Tulon..."

"Do it," he growled, moving behind her to force her if need be.

When she complied, he growled. Now this was a sight he could look at for days. Her short spiky hair provided him with a perfect view of her long neck, graceful back and an ass he could worship forever. Her breasts, still swollen from her climax, swayed under her.

"Tulon, I don't think—"

"I don't want you to think. I want you to enjoy," he said through gritted teeth. Pleasuring her was slow torture for him.

Pushing her down onto her arms, her ass rose up higher to meet him. Her core was still dripping with her sex, so he moved up to lick her cheeks. Then he smacked her.

"Ooh," she said, alarmed and excited all at once.

This was the Rowena he had glimpsed. Another smack, followed by nips and kisses on her flushed ass had her moaning and squirming for more.

When both of her cheeks were pink from his handprints, only then did he give in to his need to feel her wet pussy muscles clench his aching cock.

Plunging deeply into her, he loved how she moved back, almost sitting on his stones. He mercilessly plunged again and again into her, almost touching her womb. Faster and faster he pumped inside her, holding her around the waist, so he could angle his cock just so.

With his other hand, he pebbled her still sensitive nub into a state of frenzied desire.

"Tulon, stop...I can't...oh mymy," said Rowena, when he slightly pinched her nub between two fingers.

Pounding into her, sweat broke out on his forehead. It was hard to keep the release he ached for at bay. He needed her to climax again, so he forced her head down to the grass, which provided him with a better angle.

Mercilessly he stroked her. Between his shaft's pounding rhythm and his fingers pebbling her nub, he knew the minute she got swept away in her own passion. She squirmed her ass against him, causing his cock to move in a circular motion that made him see red.

"Tulon," she screamed, arching her back and ass more into him, as she strained again for release. Her muscles clenched around his shaft and that was it. He swore he saw stars, as he gave in to the powerful need to spill his seed deep within her.

The hum of energy filled them. His magic soared around them, almost blinding him with the knowledge of it. Now it all began to make sense.

The memories of the night of his *thrush* crashed into his mind and he almost bellowed with the realization that he had been duped. While the need for revenge ran wild in his veins, he had taken a challenge oath and he meant to fulfill it.

Lying next to Rowena on the crushed, warm grass, he realized this Maida woman had captured his heart, soul and his body. He wanted more than the physical aspect they shared. He wanted all of her. And he wouldn't settle for anything else.

"Rowena, I need to tell you something," he said, propping himself up on his elbows so he could watch her reaction.

He watched as she turned over, her face and chest still flushed from her passion, her eyes still closed. Only once she opened them did he have a moment of hesitation.

What would she think, once he admitted he had accepted the challenge that Zickal had offered without giving thought to her needs. *Probably the worst.* He hated himself all over again.

"What?" she asked, her eyes cloudy with desire, as she looked up at him with innocence.

"I...um..." He didn't know where to start.

Her hand on his cheek touched him deeply. He would rather walk through fire than tell her the truth.

"I need to tell you something. I accepted a challenge from Zickal that you're not going to like. Honestly, at the time it seemed the only thing I could do to ensure we get off Mount Atrophe alive. What I have to say, you're not going to like."

"Then just say it, Tulon."

"Fine. The challenge was that whoever made you climax three times won you and freedom." *There, I said it. Now she's going to blow up at me and leave.*

"Um, let me get this straight. Whoever, meaning either you or the prince, right?" she said, partially sitting up on her elbows to observe him.

Tulon nodded, not liking where this was going.

"Whoever could make me climax three times won freedom...um, that's interesting...so, by my calculations, you still owe me one." There was a wicked gleam in her bright sky-blue eyes.

Tulon gulped. That wasn't the reaction he had expected. Once again his Rowena had surprised him. Having bared the terrible choice he had accepted, she rose to the challenge.

"Are you up to it...?" She slowly slid her eyes down the length of him.

Immediately, his cock jumped to attention under her scrutiny.

"Because, by the Saints, I want out of this place."

"Are you asking me to pleasure you again, Rowena?" asked Tulon, knowing full well his shaft was already throbbing with desire as he thought about what he'd really like to do to her.

She nodded, lying once again in the grass. "Pretty please."

Her enticement caused all the hairs on his body to stand on end. He planned on not only pleasuring her, but he planned to claim all of her once and for all. He was about to brand her as his and to hell with the consequences.

"Turn over," he demanded.

"Again," she replied saucily, doing as he demanded.

"I plan to make all of you mine," he said, licking her earlobe. Her shuddering shiver delighted him.

"Then do it," she demanded, turning her face to give him one of her sexy, do what you will smiles that melted his heart.

"With pleasure," he replied,

With his cock still wet from their previous lovemaking and now once again thick and hard, he slid it along the crack of her ass. She squirmed against him, a little unsure. He didn't want to talk about what he was doing, he just needed to do it—mark her as his. Brand all of her. Taking his cock in his hand, he positioned it at her other virginal opening and then slowly inched his way into her ass.

If she was going to protest, this would be the time. Instead, she oohed and aahed, as the new sensation filled her. Still sliding into her slowly, he moved a finger lower to stroke her sensitive nub. Then he couldn't help himself. He plunged in, her tight opening giving way for his large cock.

He waited, letting her body get used to the hard feel of him.

"Move inside me," she said, urging him on as she leaned more into him.

That was the only encouragement he needed. Pulling out of her tight ass he plunged in again, and again, the entire time his fingers tormenting her nub and her wet pussy below. She met his thrust by arching back into him, again and again, picking up the tempo. Then he moved his hands to her aroused breasts and tweaked her nipples hard, loving the feel of their weight in his hands.

He heard her cry out his name as she climaxed for the third time and he thanked the Saints he held back. Only once he felt the shudders run wild through her body did he let loose. His throaty cry of release shocked him. No woman had ever made him feel like Rowena had. That realization rocked his world. He knew, without a doubt, he would never let her go. She was his. She simply didn't know it yet.

Then he bit her hard, forcing a part of his essence, the magic that ran in his cells, into her system. He planned on making her his forever.

"Tulon, what have you done?" she asked.

"You are mine. I have made you what I am," he said, finally falling wearily to the grass.

"And what is that?" she asked, turning onto her back to lie next to him on the grass.

"This," he said, holding out his hands to let the magic flow through his system. He felt the moment when his cells started to vibrate with the change. In a flash, he was whole—a Centaur, once again.

Next to him stood Rowena, his forever in her new Centaur form. She was breathtaking. A sleek chestnut brown. She was a good two heads smaller than him. He watched in awe as she took the time to examine herself, lifting first one leg, then the other.

"By the Saints, this is amazing. I can't believe how powerful I feel. What did you do?" she asked, trying to get used to prancing on all four legs.

"I gave you a part of my magic. Without you, Rowena, I would never have discovered the power that was within me. I need you. Will you stay with me? We can flash back into human form, but this is what I really am. This is what you are. A Centaur," he admitted.

"This is amazing. It's like a dream come true. I can't believe it. You're saying I can become this at will and then simply flash back to being Maida," she replied, edging her way cautiously toward him as she steadied herself with her long legs like a new foal learning to walk.

"Tulon, whether you are man or Centaur, I will always want to be with you. I can't imagine my life without you."

Tulon felt his heart swell. Those were the words he needed to hear. Words he burned to believe.

"Great, then let's go. We still have to get Felicia to her kin before it's too late for her, so I do believe I'll flash us there," he said, grinning.

"I thought you couldn't flash from here," said Rowena.

"I couldn't then, but I have to admit that the power of our lovemaking has awakened the magic within me. So take my hand, Rowena, and let's be on our way." He flanked his body next to hers, enjoying the feel of her small hairs bristling against his.

"With pleasure," she replied.

Chapter Eleven

Rowena was in complete awe of her new form. Never in her wildest dreams would she have imagined this to be possible. She felt powerful, wild, and yet utterly feminine.

As a Centaur, she had the long graceful body of a horse. Her hair was light brown, with just a hint of red, but what she loved most was the feel of her upper body. She was still very much the same, except that her hair had grown to the length of a horse's mane, and her breasts looked slightly bigger. She wasn't embarrassed by her naked chest. Instead, she reveled in it.

There had been a slight burning she felt when Tulon had flashed her into a Centaur, but otherwise she felt no discomfort.

Wow, talk about the reconstruction of DNA. Her rational, scientific brain marveled that she could become this, while her heart knew without a doubt that this was what she wanted. She knew inherently she was still Maida, but different. She felt it to her core.

The best part was knowing she would never be affected by the Maida fertility curse again. Sex was now guilt-free.

Tulon had given a part of his essence to make her what she was. It was his gift to her. That cemented her feelings for him more than all of his lovemaking, which had been wild, wicked and beyond her previously limited fantasies. Now, by the Saints, she looked forward to what other lovemaking positions he had in mind. So far, he had exceeded all of her expectations.

In a blink, they were flashed back to where the Pegcentaurs were. The scene that greeted them caused Rowena to weep.

The knowledge that Felicia, the young Betikhan, was dead pooled all her lovely feelings into a dark pit.

How dare I be happy, when we failed Felicia. Grief overwhelmed her.

Part of her still couldn't believe they were too late for Felicia. But there she lay, high up on a traditional burial mound about to be burnt as an offering to the Saints. She was dead. Even though she hadn't known the young Betikhan long, she had felt an affinity for her. They had shared the same potentially tragic end. Only thing was she had found her much-needed release and more.

"How long ago did this happen?" she overheard Tulon asking Rusty.

"An hour ago. She started to slowly decline after you left and then she went into a spasm, lost consciousness and, about an hour ago, her heart stopped beating," replied his friend, clearly grief-stricken. "We didn't know what to do, so I decided that we should follow our traditions."

"I think I can bring her back," said Tulon, quietly to Rusty.

With Rowena's new, sensitive hearing, she could clearly hear every word he said. Joy crept into her heart. *Tulon can save her, but how?*

"How?" she asked, flanking them.

"Rowena, I can't guarantee it will work, but I think we should try," said Tulon.

"We've got company," said Hilt, the young Pegcentaur, coming to stand between them.

Rowena's eyes grew round. She couldn't believe what she was seeing and she couldn't believe just how off their timing was. A group of about a hundred Betikhans marched toward them, all heavily armed with bows and arrows and small axes.

"Give me a minute," said Rusty, moving to intercept the group.

Once he left, Rowena assessed the situation. "What will happen if you can't bring her back?"

"Then it will be all-out war between the Betikhans and Pegcentaurs, which will spill over into the forest to become a war between the two-legged creatures and the four-legged. Betikhans hate four-leggeds. Years ago, they fought against each other and only recently a shaky truce was accepted. Things don't look good."

"I trust you, Tulon. We will bring her down and, by the Saints, you had better deliver, because if not, things aren't going to be pretty," said Rusty, returning quickly as he ordered two Pegcentaurs to bring Felicia down off the burial mound.

Rowena ached to go to her friend, but she couldn't. She watched as a small group of Betikhans moved forward to see Felicia for themselves. They appeared grief-stricken. She quirked an eye at Tulon, trying to figure out what was going on.

Rusty came to stand by her side. "That's just great. It seems that your young Betikhan friend is their long-lost princess. Things are officially really bad. I knew I was going to regret saving your ass, Tulon."

"Princess," whispered Rowena, hoping for a miracle to make everything right for all of them.

"I need a quiet place to work," demanded Tulon.

"We will not leave her," said a handsome young Betikhan as he moved forward from the group to glare at them. "What did you do to her?"

Rowena gulped. The Betikhan was alarmingly handsome and fierce. His face was tattooed with black ink, as were his arms. He was regal and menacing all at once. "We didn't do anything to her. We were trying to find you," she snapped, wanting to set the record straight.

Quickly, Tulon stepped forward to tell the Betikhan how they had met Felicia and why they were looking after her. A look of rage passed over the young Betikhan's face, but then as fast as it came, it went.

"You can save her?" the Betikhan asked.

"I will try," said Tulon.

"I will not leave her," replied the Betikhan.

"Rusty, can you get everyone to give us some space? Tulon, let him stay. You said we were racing against time, so let's just do it. By the way, what do I do?" asked Rowena.

Tulon moved closer to her. "Take my hand. No matter what, don't let go. I will need to wield the magic into her cells. It could be painful."

Rowena did as he commanded, anxious to get things moving.

"I will lend you my power as well," offered the young Betikhan, kneeling down beside Felicia.

"So be it," replied Tulon, grasping Rowena's hand tightly. "Don't let go."

Rowena nodded. More than anything, she hoped he could pull off this miracle. The repercussions wouldn't be good if he didn't.

A slow hum of energy sizzled the hairs on her body as the magic arced its way from Tulon through her and into Felicia. Rowena watched spellbound as Felicia's body rose up with the force of the energy as it moved into her body. A red haze surrounded the four of them. She spared a quick glance at Tulon and noted the sweat pouring off his brow as he focused on the task at hand.

A warm tingle traveled from her legs to her mound, then up to her scalp. Then pain, the likes of which almost brought her to her four knees slammed deep into her. Through sheer willpower, she held tightly to Tulon's hand.

Instinctively, she knew that if she let go, the magic he was pouring into Felicia would evaporate. She felt Tulon's arm muscles bunch as he concentrated on forcing the power to do his bidding. Red streaks of blood now marred his face. Yet still he pushed beyond his abilities. He did not let on that his body was on fire, like hers.

This was the Tulon she had come to admire. He was brave, courageous and, more than that, he was determined and selfless to those in need. She showered him with love, wielding her own magic—letting him feel her emotion, hoping it would lend him strength.

Then a blue haze filtered through the red and she saw Felicia open her eyes, heard her take a breath of air and come fully awake. Slowly, Tulon lowered her body back to the green grass.

"What happened?" she asked, sitting up on her elbows, her eyes wide with fear as she took in the sight that greeted her.

"Don't be alarmed, Felicia," said Rowena, forcing her large Centaur body to kneel. "Tulon fixed you and you're going to be okay." She noted how Felicia looked at her, bewildered. "You could also say he fixed me," she said, smiling.

Then Felicia turned her head. She looked the young male Betikhan up and down and then lazily smiled at him. "Who are you?" she asked, her voice husky with its suggestiveness.

"I am your mate," replied the male Betikhan. Then he promptly kissed her, making sure she knew he intended to claim her.

Rowena blushed. Intimate displays of affection still caused her to bristle, but she was slowly getting used to the ways of the wild. She let Tulon drag her away from Felicia.

Then a huge cry of delight filled the meadow when Tulon informed the Betikhans that Felicia, their lost princess, was okay.

Rowena ached to be alone with Tulon. There were too many prying eyes watching their every move, but before she had a chance to say anything, the creature she despised materialized in front of her.

"I can't believe you cheated," said Zickal, flashing into human form in front of them.

"Cheat, me?" chimed Tulon.

Rowena didn't like the hard, calculated look on Tulon's face. She watched as he flashed into human form next to Zickal. He looked like a man bent on revenge, but over what?

"You want to talk about cheating. Why don't you tell everyone, Zickal, how you became Prince of the Forest? I'm sure they would all like to hear the truth for a change."

Zickal snorted as he marched closer to Tulon. "What are you talking about?"

Rowena watched as Tulon faced Zickal.

Through gritted teeth, Tulon told everyone within hearing range how Zickal had tricked him into sleeping on the *ovata*, the marked black stone that was off-limits to Centaurs going through the *thrush*.

The *ovata* was known for its ability to suck the magic from those who touch it and twist its power to those who stand within range. Zickal had tricked Tulon into sleeping on the black stone and then had siphoned off his magic to filter it into his being so he could flash into the unicorn, the one and only creature that was Prince of the Forest.

Since the previous prince had died a decade ago, every creature in the forest had been awaiting the return of a new prince.

"This is what they were really waiting for. I am your true prince," stated Tulon, flashing himself into a unicorn. Black as a starless night, he stood regally proud before them. His horn was polished white and its brilliance shone around everyone in the meadow.

Rowena watched as every creature knelt to pay homage to Tulon. They all knew his words were true. There was no hesitation. He was the real Prince of the Forest.

Chapter Twelve

When next Rowena looked, Zickal was gone. "Where did he go?"

Instantly Tulon flashed back into his Centaur form. He bowed his head in acknowledgement of the creatures kneeling before him.

"I am Tulon, your rightful prince. And this is Rowena, my mate," he said, once again taking her hand. Before the kneeling assembly of Pegcentaurs and Betikhans, he gallantly kissed it. Then he flashed them away to a more private place.

"Prince," squeaked Rowena, flashing herself into human form. *Wow, I'm actually getting used to this power.*

She watched, still in awe, as Tulon took human form. "Is that so bad?" he asked, licking his lips, as he lay down on a bed of tempra flowers, his muscled body gleaming in the sunlight.

"I certainly hope so," she replied wickedly, as she knelt between his legs.

Without preamble, she took the long, hard length of his cock deep into the recesses of her mouth.

Rowena knew the fertility curse was broken for her. She would never have to worry about that again. She had felt Tulon's magic heal her from within. Scientifically, she longed to discover how he or the magic had done it.

She wished with her soul she could heal all the Maida women who sought fertility or those that faced the ticking time bomb of the dreaded curse. But at the moment, with the tip of him teasing her mouth, she burned feverishly to have him wedged deep inside her body.

As if he read her mind, he bucked his cock deep into her mouth, once and then twice. Then he withdrew and captured her waist to turn her around so that once again she was on her knees, begging for his pleasure. When he plunged deeply into her aching, wet pussy, she almost wept from the sheer pleasure of their joining.

"Will you submit to my desires?" he asked, forcing her head down so that her cheek was resting on the wildflowers, so he could lick her neck, nip her shoulder blades and smack her ass.

Ohh the delicious things he will do to me. She reached around to grasp his ass with one hand so he could pound faster and deeper within her weeping core.

Without a doubt, Rowena knew that life with Tulon would never be boring and that he would ram her as often and in as many ways as he liked. That she leapt to his challenge and throbbed for release told her she had finally found her mate and she would let him love her wild.

"Come for me, Rowena," he demanded, once again smacking her pink, sensitive ass.

"Yes," she shouted, as she bucked hard against him, pushing up from her knees so that he could ram her, brand her and have his way with her.

When his hand snaked around to her front to tightly pinch her nipples, she knew she couldn't hold off any longer. She loved the feeling of how her inner muscles milked his cock.

She felt the moment when she reached heaven and beyond, and she loved how he followed suit, his hot seed spurting deep into her.

This she knew she would never tire of.

"Love me wild, always," she rasped, her body drained of all its energy, as Tulon gently lowered her to the warm flower petals.

"With pleasure," he replied, already claiming her mouth for a kiss, as his hands once again teased her still throbbing pussy.

Renee Field can be reached at www.reneefield.com[1]

When not writing, Renee is promoting other authors on StoryFinds.com, a site she founded in 2012 to help support Indie authors.

Renee loves to write a variety of genres. She writes erotic romance for Ellora's Cave, & HQN Spice Briefs and sensual paranormal romance as an Indie author. Field also writes nitty gritty young adult and paranormal young adult romance novels under the pen name Renee Pace (www.reneepace.com).

Renee calls Halifax, Nova Scotia, Canada home and loves her view of the Atlantic Ocean. She is a member of Romance Writers' of America, and her local Romance Writers of Atlantic Canada. She juggles work, four children and is a firm believer in soul-mates and the power of the sea.

Renee loves to hear from fans.

Follow her on Facebook at https://www.facebook.com/ReneeFieldRomanceAuthor

Twitter @pararomance

Email: renee@reneefield.com

Other Books:

Titan Series:

Rapture, Titan series Book 1

Bliss, Titan series Book 2

Romance Siren series:

Claiming the Temptress (novella) (HQN Spice Briefs)

Claiming Poseidon's Heart (erotic romance) *Claiming A Siren's Heart* (erotic romance)

A Siren's Wish (erotic romance)

What to Read After FSOG: The Gemstone Collection (WTRAFSOG Book 7)

Witch Me Good (Sexy Salem Witch Stories Book 1)

---

1.   http://www.reneefield.com

Spice Me Up (contemporary romance)
Darklander Lovers Series (erotic paranormal romance)
Be My Vampire Tonight (Darklander Lovers, Book One)
Be My Werecat Tonight (Darklander Lovers, Book Two)
Be My Warlock Tonight (Darklander Lovers, Book Three)
Contemporary Romance:
Embrace (sweet contemporary romance novella)
Summer Heat (new adult romance)

Don't miss out!

Visit the website below and you can sign up to receive emails whenever Renee Field publishes a new book. There's no charge and no obligation.

https://books2read.com/r/B-A-HRN-LPIR

BOOKS 2 READ

Connecting independent readers to independent writers.

Did you love *Love Me Wild*? Then you should read *Be My Vampire Tonight*[2] by Renee Field!

Bidding on a masked man at an auction is all for a good cause, but what happens when he turns out to be a vampire who has the power to unleash the wild woman lying dormant inside you?

As a Darklander vampire, Mitch has spent a century living in a bleak world, but all that changes when he sees Tina. The beast living within Mitch wants to stake his claim. Mitch knows taking Tina's virginity will change her forever, but try explaining that to a woman whose passion cannot be denied.

Tina holds the key to his freedom, but Mitch will be damned forever before he turns her over as a slave for his master.

Book one in the Darklander Lovers series.

---

2. https://books2read.com/u/3RoMDG

3. https://books2read.com/u/3RoMDG

Read more at www.reneefield.com.

Also by Renee Field

A Warriors of Maida Novella
Love Me Wild
Love Me Tender
Love Me Strong
Love Me Wild

Darklander Lovers
Be My Warlock Tonight
Be My Vampire Tonight
Be My Werecat Tonight

Elemental Love
Heart of Mine

Riverton Cove series
Embrace

Titan series
Rapture
Bliss

Standalone
Claiming A Siren's Heart
Claiming Poseidon's Heart
A Siren's Wish
Fairy Cursed
Summer Heat
Queen of Dragons
Summer Heat
Electrify Me

Watch for more at www.reneefield.com.

About the Author

Renee loves to write a variety of genres. She writes for HQN Spice Briefs and also writes sensual paranormal romance, and contemporary romance as an Indie author. Field also writes nitty gritty young adult and paranormal young adult romance novels under the pen name Renee Pace. Renee calls Halifax, Nova Scotia, Canada home and loves her view of the Atlantic Ocean. She is a member of Romance Writers' of America, and her local Romance Writers of Atlantic Canada. She juggles work, four children and is a firm believer in soul-mates and the power of the sea.

Renee loves to hear from fans. She can be reached by email at reneefieldauthor@gmail.com

Read more at www.reneefield.com.